The Rise of the Bloods From Dark Beginnings

K A HAMBLY

Acknowledgements

Special thanks to Craig, Paige and Danny.

Without friends like these and their support, this book would not have been possible.

Ceri, Kellie, Mick, Julie, Fi, Barbara, Dena, Leanne, Sonia.

CHAPTER ONE

I took a deep breath and sighed. It wasn't as if I needed to breathe but it just seemed natural to do it anyway. After all, I was descended from the humans; maybe, just maybe there was still a trace of humanity left in me somewhere. I laughed to myself, as I knew it was just wishful-thinking on my part. I looked out of the small window from my wooden cabin. The days were long but the nights were tedious and lonely. I had somehow become used to my mundane existence but lately there was a longing in me for change. After the morning I had out hunting for food with father it looked like change was swiftly on the horizon. Father had been unusually quiet all day. I sensed something was preying on his mind. I wondered, could this have been what we had been preparing for all these years.

'Jyrki...Jyrki, where the hell are you?'
I heard my friend William hollering at me from the ground. I snapped out of my self-pity and looked down from the window.

'Didn't you hear the horn? Amroath has ordered everyone to tear down their quarters,' he yelled
I hadn't. I was deep in thought, almost in an hypnotic state.

For a few moments, his words didn't seem to sink in. Until I looked up and saw the rest of the clan leaving their homes. I shot up from the floor and grabbed my jacket that was hanging by a nail on the door almost tearing it in the process and climbed down the ladder. It was becoming dark, so I reached for the lantern on the branch and skipped the last few steps. The snow was thick on the ground. Which wasn't unusual for Finland this time of year. I waited nervously in the falling snow as the events unfolded before me. I looked on in horror at the destruction of what was once my home. The Cabins were being abandoned at such speed, and torn down with bare hands to destroy all evidence of our existence. The protection of the grand Fir trees that encircled us held us together no more. I knew there was much worse to come.

'Jyrki! Wait there a moment; I need to speak with you.' I heard a familiar voice from behind me.

I swerved around and held the lantern up. It was Draven, my brother, running towards me from the lake.

'Looks like our old man has come to his senses and we're getting the hell out of here,' I said quite sternly. I was half hoping the latter were true. Two hundred years on these Aaland Islands and people were now getting too close for comfort.

Draven placed a firm hand on my shoulder and at once, I sensed something was very wrong.

'What's wrong with you?' I said, feeling quite defensive. 'I haven't seen you for days, where have you been?'

He looked at me with a worried expression on his face. 'There's something I've been meaning to give you for safekeeping.'

For a moment I hesitated to say anything, as I could sense there was a lot more going on with him than he would let on to me. His long black hair blew in a gust of wind; revealing a gash to his forehead which he tried to conceal from me.

'How did that happen to your head? Just tell me what is going on with you, please?'

He shook his head, refusing to answer my question. I noticed a few specks of snow nestled onto his black cloak and a coldness in the air I hadn't felt for ages.

'There's something darker coming for us.'

His words sent a chill through me. Subconsciously I knew there was great danger ahead of us. I just didn't want to admit it to myself. Dusk settled behind him and the silvery light of the full moon changed the hue of the snow to a subtler blue. He reached inside his cloak and pulled out Father's khopesh sword.

'This serpent's sword is yours now; you must take care of it.'

I smiled half-heartedly, waiting for him to say it was a joke. His expression didn't falter under the orange glow. Now I knew I had real cause for concern, as the sword had never left Draven's side since Father had given it to him.

'Take it, it's yours.'

He held the bronzed handle of a coiled serpent toward me and waited for me to take it.

'I've a bad feeling that things are going to get crazy around here soon, and as you know I've won a few wars in my time with this, but now it needs to be with the Chosen One.'

'Stop talking like that, we don't know if it's the prophecy yet.' Hastily, I took the sword from his hands and placed it in my backpack. They were the only means of weapons we ever fought with, despite our little knowledge that the outside world had long since changed. It was now the tail end of the twentieth century and I was feeling anxious about the sudden turn of events that could propel us into a whole new world.

'Over here, now!'

It was Amroath, our Father, shouting to us from across the compound. We both swerved our heads at the sense of immediacy in his voice. I drew another breath in anticipation of what news he had to share.

Words didn't have to manifest from anyone's lips. It was obvious from the dark mood what was about to take place. I brushed my long black hair away from my face and stood in front of father, Draven joined the rest of the clan who were already prepping their weapons. They all turned to look at me. I somehow felt a sense of responsibility for their lives.

'It's time son.'

I turned to look at Father whose ashen face must've aged a few years in those split seconds. He didn't have to say anything else, I knew what he meant.

'It's the prophecy isn't it?'

Father took my hand and placed an Ankh into my palm. I clenched it tightly. Part of me couldn't bear to look at it because I knew by father handing me the one thing that kept us all shielded from the sun, he was placing their lives in mortal danger. Mardok, a prophet in Ancient Egypt had given him the Ankh. He had warned him that when the day came to hand over the Ankh to the chosen one, all his protection would be lost. It was written in the prophecy, he said.

'There was word less than an hour ago, the Others have detected us. You must leave now! You know what you are meant to do; we have been over this for many many years.'

His voice was strangely calm for someone who was about to face the unknown.

'So I leave you all here to perish at the hands of these... things?' I raged. 'Not likely, I'm staying here to fight with you.'

Amroath was becoming rather annoyed with me.

'Look at me,' he said as he grabbed the sleeve of my jacket.

I stood before him and looked into his eyes. There was no bitterness or remorse for all the things he had done. Not even a touch of regret for what he was. I was in awe of him, and proud to have him as my Father. He bent his head slightly, allowing some silvery strands of hair to fall into his face. He clenched me tightly and gave me the last piece of advice I would ever receive.

'Even immortals meet their match one day. Nothing is forever. We were sworn to protect the Ankh and now the time has come to do just that...I trust in you Jyrki, just as the ancients did all those years ago.' Knowing better than to argue with my Father, I held my peace.

'I guess you didn't become the New Blood elder for your people skills?' I managed a wry laugh.

'I hardly think we could be classed as people, do you?' he smiled.

'Amroath!' William yelled. 'They're getting closer. My guess is they'll be here at dawn.'

It was arctic cold and the sky was grey and heavy with blizzards. I placed the Ankh around my neck and mentally prepared myself for the task ahead.

'Jyrki, we'll see each other again, I'm sure.'

Draven was acting as a brother would, but I could tell he was putting on a brave face just for me. It had always been the same way since we were children. I stood watching the clan as they handed out swords and spears to each other. Their silence was ripping me apart inside. Draven stooped down and gave me a farewell hug. I knew then that this was it. I gripped him tightly. 'I will make you proud, I promise.'

'I know you will, just stay safe until this battle is all over, okay.'

'I will. I'm going to miss you,' I wept.

I wiped the tears from my eyes and glanced up at Father who stood beside us gazing affectionately at his two sons for what would be the last time.

'There's not a lot of time, William can hear them approaching. Now Jyrki, you must do as I have asked you and keep the Ankh safe from the humans, and hopefully one day it will save us wherever we may be.'

'I give you my word,' I whispered.

I gave father a farewell hug and then picked up my holdhall. Just moments ago, I was secretly hoping for change now it was here I wasn't sure if it was what I really wanted. For a moment, I stood and peered around at the vastness of the forest, a place I had called home for so long. Now, instead of the exquisite beauty of the lakes and trees, all I saw were the dark shadows of our past coming back to haunt us.
As I turned to look at Father one last time, I saw he had tears in his eyes. He wiped them away with his thick leathery hand and whispered for me to go. Draven met my gaze and nodded encouragingly.

'You'll realise in time what that thing can do,' I heard Father shout, but I was halfway through the forest by now. I paused for a brief moment and inhaled. My senses became heightened as I left the safe zone.

'No time for snacks,' I thought to myself as I saw a hare scurry into its burrow.
I picked up speed as I reached the mountain. The little light reflecting from the snow helped steer my way to the highest peak. I found a place to sit on the rocky edge where I tried to gather my thoughts for a while; still I had no idea where I was going all I knew was that I had to get away from Finland without anyone asking too many questions. Yet I was torn between running back down there to help my family, but Father would not have been pleased. Our fates were worlds apart right now.

It felt like another lifetime just waiting for the final battle to burn out. I knew we didn't stand a chance against The Others. From what father had told me, they were far too superior to our old-fashioned ways. My mood was sombre and I was craving blood. I couldn't find the strength within me to move, so I chose to endure my hunger for a while longer. The night-time passed by as slowly as it ever did, but just as the last glimmer of hope diminished there was a break in the clouds and the sun began to peek through. It was a new dawn and something within me told me it was all over. It had to be. The Others would only fight at daybreak as they knew the clan would be at their most vulnerable. I checked my chest to make sure the Ankh was still there. 'All for this?' I whispered as I held the silver Amulet in my ice-cold hands. I felt so much hatred towards it. It was the reason why we ended up in this mess in the first place. As I got up to leave, I sensed a small squirrel behind the rock I was sitting on. If I was quick enough I should be able to catch him. With a quick sudden movement, I leapt behind the rock and caught the creature by its tail. The food was enough to satisfy me until I could find something with a little more blood. Feeling a little more energised than earlier I made the decision of walking back to the compound. I knew I shouldn't go back to the forest but I felt I needed to say my goodbyes before the sun was at its peak. I had minutes to spare. I was dreading what I would see.

I made my way down from the mountain through the uneven path, relying on my natural navigational skills to find my way back. Most of the compound was over shadowed by the mass of trees that was heavily laden with snow. With any luck, if someone were alive they would be safe for a while, I hoped. The gentle twittering of a song thrush brought a welcome relief to my ears. I braced myself behind the trunk of the tree as I looked for traces of the enemy. Nothing. They must've long gone by now I would've thought, in search of me.

I glanced around once more to be certain before trekking slowly down the embankment. No sooner had I reached the bottom, I could smell the bloodshed that engulfed my lungs like smoke. I keeled over and retched. As my head brushed against the snow, my nostrils flared as I opened my eyes to see their blood splattered in the pure crestfallen snow. Consumed with grief, I somehow forced myself off the ground and walked towards the carnage. My hands were now shaking as I desperately removed the bodies one by one from the pile in hope to find someone alive. The image before me pained me deeply. I stopped for a moment to take it all in but the sight of William's lifeless body stretched out on the snow before me was all too much. My body went limp and I sank to the floor in despair.

'Why?' I screamed. 'This wasn't meant to happen!' I was aware of my voice echoing throughout the compound. I cupped my hands over my face and sat rocking back and forth, when I came to realise the stinging sensation of the cold on my fingers was slowly easing away by the warmth of the sun.

'Oh no, please no,' I whispered.
As I removed my hands from my face, I looked up towards the sky and saw the sun was almost at its zenith.

I quickly got to my feet and began searching for Father and Draven, but time wasn't on my side. As I was about to bend down to pick up William, I saw at the corner of my eye the sun rays hovering over the bodies and stood watching in horror as one by one they turned to dust.

For it was in that very moment, I knew I was the last Vampire.

CHAPTER TWO

I had to get away as quickly as possible. The compound offered me no protection now. Our agreement with the ancient prophet to keep our identity secret would be broken in the instant we showed ourselves to the humans. How this had happened, I do not know. My suspicion was it had something to do with Draven, as he was always leaving the compound at night-time, but sitting here looking at their ashes blowing in amongst the dusting of snow I had to accept the fact I'd probably never know for sure.

I felt the snow gently caressing my pale, grief stricken face. It was now time to leave. I picked myself up from the floor and wrapped my coat around me for comfort. Everything had happened so fast and unexpectedly. I don't think I fully appreciated the magnitude of the task ahead. The last hour of my life was like a blur I cared not to think about right now. I had to be strong and do what Father had asked. It was the only way to keep their memory alive.

As I turned to walk away, I heard a snapping of a branch behind me. 'The Others,' I muttered to myself. It was possible. A slight rustle of the tree branches behind me struck me with fear. I dared not move and show them I was initiating a fight, instead, I tried to stay calm to avoid letting the vampire loose. I didn't want to take any chances in case it was human. My eyes suddenly became alerted to the tree in front me. The snow began falling off its branches by the quick, sharp movement of something behind it. This wasn't human, neither was it another vampire. Then what in the hell was it.

Should I call out to it? I sensed it was not an animal of the woods, but it was an animal of some kind. I decided to hone in on my vampire instinct to be certain. As I inhaled the smell of their blood, I became acutely aware of their presence all around me, concealing themselves behind the trees. Were they playing tricks with me? Were they the ones who had killed my family? So many questions went through my head I began to feel disorientated and weak with hunger.

'Who are you? What have you come here for?' I called out.
There was no answer. I was becoming rather frustrated and angry. Then I suddenly realised my thoughts were being replaced by the answers

they were giving.

'We are the others,' a male voice spoke with utmost authority.

'What's happening?' I yelled out. Startled by their presence in my mind I placed my hands on my head and frantically paced about in the snow. They were inside my head and I didn't like it.

'Show yourselves to me!' I yelled.

The human-like voice remained calm. 'No. Not right now.'

'Why not? Why did you kill my family? Who sent you here?' I seethed, casting a critical eye over the trees.

'All in due time Jyrki, all in due time. I can tell you what you need to know for now but the rest will soon follow in the most unexpected of places and people Be aware though there are people searching for you and the Ankh and when you meet them you will know whether to trust them or not. Stay true to yourself and stay in hiding. You will know when the time is right to leave. We have to go now, but we'll be watching you.'

'That's it, you're leaving? So you're not going to kill me too?'

'No, it was never our intention to. You are far too important Jyrki.' Then they were gone as quickly as they came and my thoughts were once again my own. Many years had now passed and there was still no sign of these creatures. I had come to believe they were what father had spoken to me about the day we were out in the woods, looking for food. He sat on a log skinning a rabbit as if he would normally, but I knew there was something else bothering him that day. He wouldn't reveal much to me when I asked but knowing how well my instinct was developed he couldn't very well lie to me either. It was a curse of the curse, as he used to call it. All he would tell me was that he had news that the clan had broken the agreement and Mardok was not happy. I wanted to question him further but I sensed he didn't really want to worry me.

Winter was now back again and Mother Nature had shielded its beauty once more with a fresh coating of snow. I loved this time of year. I sat on the tree branch and whistled a song I had heard a while ago. It was an old Finnish folk song, which had struck a chord with me. I breathed in some of the chill air and rested my head against the trunk. Many nights I have spent gazing up at the sky. The bluish tint served as a canvas to the map of the heavens. I think I knew every star that graced the sky as they shone and flickered above me. I continued to keep my gaze on the snowy mountain top ahead as I knew something very special was approaching. A ray of majestic green and yellow lights swathed towards me. I smiled and sat reveling in its beauty. I must've seen these Northern Lights, or Revontulet as they are fondly known in these parts, so many times, but every time was always like the first.

Dawn broke, bringing with it the sound of heavy machinery and humans. I sat upright on the branch and looked over the forest. 'Damn,' I had heard right. They were coming to tear down the trees in preparation to build a road that would connect the two villages either side of me. I jumped down, landing perfectly on my feet and frantically gathered up my things, which didn't really amount to much for a 200-year lifespan, but I was an immortal who had a purpose at least, so I didn't feel I had any right to whine. Apart from having to seek blood and learning to suppress my urge for the taste of human, I didn't know how much better life could get anyway. This was all I knew. After leaving the safety of the compound in the Aaland Islands, humans became far more interesting. I had never met one before let alone spoken to one, which made entering into their world a far more difficult move for me. I didn't know if I had the strength within me to resist the urge for their blood, but I had to try.

Since my family had been gone, I have travelled all over Finland, preferring the safety of its dark and enchanting forests to the cities. Yet, I knew the day would arrive when I had to venture out into the world to protect the Ankh, and that time was now. Something was calling me to a distant land.

I preferred to travel at night, so I was particularly thrown back when I had no choice but to leave Ivalo at the break of dawn. The humans were about to tear down the forest and I didn't think finding me in amongst it would be a good thing for either of us.

It took me six days to travel to Lake Pielinen. I usually stopped at daybreak to rest and eat. My diet consisted of anything I could find wandering around the woods at the time. I felt as long as I kept the demon happy, I wouldn't shift into my alter ego so quickly.

It was dawn when I reached the lake. Due to the mist, I had not noticed the wooden bridge at the other end of the island, so instead I chose to row the small boat I had found. I felt it was a much safer option to be away from the humans I heard on the mainland.

There was a slight breeze that harbored a Nordic chill in the air. Not one to depend on the function of breathing, I stopped rowing and inhaled. The air was crisp and fresh which made the sweet scent of human blood too irresistible to miss. Where was this human, I wondered. All I hoped was that they stayed well away from me whilst I weaned myself from the taste.

I began rowing again listening to the gentle swish of the water beneath me. My mind was relaxed and free of all the demonic chatter when I felt a jolt as the boat bumped into the land. I snapped out of my thoughts and placed the oars inside the boat. With the rope, I tied the boat to the post of the small wooden jetty and climbed out. The mist soon cleared and the island revealed itself to me. It was quiet and didn't seem to inhabit any humans, but the stench still wafted over from the island opposite. I knew this was a great place to be while I prised myself off the taste. It was the only way in which I could prepare myself for the wider world.

After exploring the island for the last hour, I had stumbled upon an old derelict farmhouse. It was in an idyllic spot, giving me a wonderful view of the water and the islands opposite. Now I had found a place for safety the hardest part was learning to control my thirst.

Days soon turned to nights, before I knew it I had been on the island for a few months. The snow had surely melted and spring was beginning to show all around, but food was becoming scarce in these parts and my hunger was becoming uncontrollable.

I felt I had no choice but to make my way back to the mainland.

CHAPTER THREE

The hunger was excruciating. I wasn't sure how much longer I was able go on without anything fresh to drink. My weak lifeless body slumped back against the tree as I stared into nothingness. I longed to feel something against my ice-cold skin. Whether it was in a moment of madness or delirium from no blood for a week but I suddenly found myself reaching inside of my jacket pocket and pulled out my pocket-knife. My hand shook from exhaustion as I reached over my forearm. Carefully I guided the tip of the   blade over the flesh. The trickling of the crimson liquid gave my body the jump-start it needed, my eyes filled with elation of the release. The numbness I had felt after losing my family slowly disappeared as I felt the charge I needed to protect the Ankh surge through my body.

 I licked a drop of my own blood from my arm and screwed my face up in disgust; I spat it out and wiped my mouth on the sleeve of my black sweater. Still, I wasn't sure what the fuck I was doing. My head was in another place. As vampire blood was so precious, to draw our own blood was a forbidden act in our circle. I shouldn't have done it but what did it matter anymore. I had no one to adhere to anyway, but after last week's fiasco, I didn't want to attempt to go into the neighbouring village. The humans were becoming a little too suspicious. Besides, Father wouldn't have been too pleased with my recent efforts for food.

 I was just about to get up from the leaf-strewn floor when I heard a few ramblers laughing in the distance. This Island wasn't safe anymore. The villagers had already begun a hunt for the killer.
'They're too close,' I mumbled to myself as I rummaged in my bag for an old t-shirt. The wound was gaping and trickling with blood. Hurriedly I wrapped the black shirt around my arm and secured it. I looked up. Over the rustling of the leaves on the trees, I could hear their voices getting closer. My hunger rendered me weak and exhausted, but there was no choice. I had to leave. A sharp pain crept up my arm making me flinch. I yelped, drawing attention to myself.
 'Did you hear that?' he said
 'Hear what?' the second man answered.
 'That sound, just then.'

'No, could've been a deer. I just saw a family of them a few yards away.'

As I bent down to pick up my bag, I caught sight of a figure in a blue jacket walking behind the bush. He was about 20 yards away. I kept low on the ground, hoping the crisp rustling of the leaves wouldn't send them my way. I waited until they carried on walking in the other direction. Now they were out of view I crept through the bush, running at an alarming speed through the forest careful not to trip up on the protruding roots of the trees along the path. I was now making my way back to the island as I felt I'd be safer until I could find a way to leave Finland. I only wished I could've controlled my hunger a bit more when I arrived on the mainland last week. I felt so guilty about killing the young man that the horror of what happened began to play out in my head again as I ran.

I never meant to hurt anyone. After witnessing my family turn to ash, I lost control of myself for a while. Selfishly, after I landed onto the mainland I found myself wandering for days on end until I reached a point where I just couldn't do it anymore. By the time I arrived at a small village I was starved and had no energy to catch anything. I was overcome by the sensuous smell of blood that lilted in the air like a fresh summer morning. I tried so hard not to let go of myself but the transformation took over me instantly. The only way to fight the demon off was to drink blood. As I inhaled my eyes latched onto a young man loading up his van with wood. I was instantly drawn and there was no turning back. The rational voice in my head had no effect whatsoever on the rest of my body. It was straight in for the kill. He didn't see me coming either thankfully. I took the plank of wood and without any remorse I smashed it across his head. As I almost drained him of his blood, I stopped, as it was far too dangerous to carry on. With all my strength, I pulled myself away from his lifeless body and instantly I could feel myself coming through again, but I was not proud of what I had done. I was disgusted with myself and spat the remainder out of my mouth before making a run for it.

This is exactly what I am still doing now, running. I paused for a brief moment and looked behind me. I was still alone but my dark thoughts were very much with me. It was only now that I had realised something; I had broken the pact my father had made with the

Ancients. That made me far worse than a killer in my eyes. I was ashamed of who I was at this point. Somehow, I had to redeem myself. An eternity of guilt and remorse was far worse than anything imaginable. My only hope of leaving these small islands to Helsinki was catching the boat some local fishermen I had been watching left at daybreak. Father had spoken about the place many times and right now, it seemed like the best option.

There was nothing I could do right now. As the boat wasn't due back for another few hours, I made the decision of going back to the old derelict farmhouse I had found for safety. No-one would find me there, I hoped. The previous owners left suddenly years ago. As far as I knew no-one had been there since. As I walked along the rocky footpath, I cowered down as the trees stretched over into an arch above my head. We were a tall family, Draven being the tallest at 6ft 6. I followed at 6ft 4. I was easily detectable and not easily forgotten. I folded my arms for comfort as the memory of them being alive lingered fresh in my head. I missed them badly.

I must've been so wrapped up in grief I wasn't paying any attention to my surroundings. I continued walking, passing the broken wooden gate of the house when I spotted some kind of metal machine parked outside. Two strange men were sitting in it watching the house.

'Shit!' I crouched down behind the crumbling wall. This was the last thing I expected to see. The two strange men got out of the doors, armed with rifles. My initial reaction would've been to kill, but I promised myself I'd change. I had to.

'Humans, they just don't know when to butt out,' I muttered.
I peered over the wall at the two men looking suspiciously around the property. One of them had a strange kind of accent, which struck me as odd.

'Take a look around the back...' The dark haired, tanned skin man ordered the tall guy with the accent.
I looked around for an escape, to my left was the path that ended with no trees for cover and to my right the garden wall, which had crumbled that would've left me exposed. I had to sit and endure it. If the worst came to the worst, I pondered...well...

'There doesn't appear to be anyone living here now. All I can see is a pile of old junk that was left by the previous occupants.'

'I wonder why she said he was here. You reckon it could've been an animal that attacked those people?' The guy with the accent said.

'Stride, I am certain he's here, but if he's gone now I just hope he turns up soon...c'mon let's get the hell out of here.'

I sat nervously behind the wall, fidgeting with the frayed ends of my sweater. I couldn't believe what I had just heard. If I'm right, which I normally was anyway, they knew of my kind. That didn't seem possible in my mind, but I didn't have much time to rationalise things in my head right now, I had to get the sword from the house quickly before they knew I was here. With no other option of waiting by the lake until dawn, I knew I had to leave right away incase they showed up again. I listened out for a bit until I heard them slam the doors and drive away through the back entrance, which joined onto the road into the village. As I took a glance over the wall and assured myself they had gone, I relaxed my chest and picked myself up from the floor.

'Time Jyrki, time,' I kept repeating to myself as I ran up to the door. I could feel myself getting into a right state. I sprinted upstairs into the small back bedroom and grabbed my bag from under the bed. Frantically, I pulled the bag open to check Draven's sword was indeed safe. Looking at it, with its missing piece cut out of the blade you wouldn't think it was anything special, but Father always swore it was forged during the Blood War and had been used to kill the vampires. My instinct told me it would be needed one day, so I placed it back in my bag and grabbed the rest of my things, mainly books. I looked around the room, afraid I had left something that could be linked to me. There was an old armchair, a pine dresser...I screwed my eyes up and walked over to the dresser. A black and white photograph of a young couple stifled my curiosity. I slung the bag over my shoulder and picked up the frame. 'So lucky,' I whispered to myself. A painful wave of emotions attacked me as it dawned on me how alone I was. I placed the photo back and picked up the book next to it. 'Irving Washington's, History of New York.' I threw the book into my bag and ran down the stairs. It was getting on for dusk, so I slammed the door shut behind me and decided I would hunt for food on my way out of the island.

I was hungry. The last meal I had was more than a week ago. Sometimes, depending on the richness of the blood, it would sustain in my system for longer, hence I could go without food for a vast amount of time. Now human blood was off the menu I decided to look for it elsewhere. I didn't have much of a choice but to turn back to rabbit food again. Still panged with guilt, I vowed never to taste the delicacy of human blood ever again. Although now that I had a taste, I knew it was going to be too difficult to resist it, which worried me greatly, as I was heading to the city.

It was almost midnight when I reached the lake. I could've been there in an instant, but I felt like taking a slower pace tonight and soak in the memories of home one last time. There was nobody around but nature's nightlife. I sat on the bank and enjoyed the simple tranquility of watching the ripples in the water, with the moonlight adding a beautiful lustre to it. I think I could've stayed here forever completely immersed in my thoughts.

'Oh fuck, what am I doing here?' I said, gritting my teeth. I clenched my bag tightly as I stood dumbstruck on the pavement. I didn't know what I was expecting to see when I got off the boat in Helsinki, but this certainly superseded my expectations. 'Don't do anything rash.' I kept repeating to myself as I saw people hurriedly pass me. Blood, I need blood, was all I could think. My lips were dry and it was getting harder to control my natural instincts. I could feel myself starting to panic, so I crossed the street to try to avoid a group of people that stood next to me.

The promise I made my father about never exposing our identity to people hung firmly in the balance. I felt like I was going to shift. I stumbled off the kerb, feeling weak and dizzy.

'Hey watch it!' a voice yelled 'You nearly hit me off my fucking bike.'

I swerved my head towards the guy on the bicycle and glared.

'You freak!' he screamed back at me as he rode off.

The voice in my head kept telling me to stay calm. If this had been somewhere else he wouldn't had stood a chance, but I had to try and fit into this mad world, I just had to. Feeling like I shouldn't have come here I sat down on the edge of the pavement and tucked my head into my hands.

'Are you alright son?' the voice called from behind me.

I turned around and looked at the slightly overweight middle-aged man standing by the shop doorway with his arms folded. My nostrils flared as I inhaled the smell of fresh meat that wafted from the door. My eyes widened and my throat yearned for some warm blood.

'Why do you ask?'

'You look like you need a good feed that's all.'

He was right. I was so weak after all the travelling I dare not take a guess at what I looked like to him.

'I don't suppose you have anything fresh, maybe with a little blood on it?' I asked as my eyes were firmly fixed on his blood stained apron.

His eyes narrowed and his grey brows knit together.

'Blood you say? What are you a wild animal?'

I sat open mouthed and thought I had landed myself in a bit of bother.

'Er, yes. I prefer my meat like that.'

I never studied human behaviour before neither had I given any thought to their reactions to me, yet judging by this guy's reaction I could sense there was fear surrounding him. Fear made people do irrational things that I knew very well, as there was still a trace of my ancestors in me. I honestly thought he knew what I was, just for a few seconds. I wasn't sure what I was doing but I felt like I was reading his emotions. It had never happened to me before. As I was about to get away from there, his frown turned to a smile.

'Sure, I'll go look out the back for you.'

I sighed with relief and walked into the shop.

Relieved he didn't question anything I stood by the counter top fiddling with the leaflets. My nerves were shot and I was starving. All I hoped for was that this food would be enough to fulfill me until I got to America.

My eyes followed him as he walked into the stock room. I tried to blot out my crazy thoughts and concentrate on getting the hell out of this city. Moments later, he walked back out with a few pound of fresh flesh he had promised. I almost lunged at him over the counter top. I was that desperately hungry.

'I don't have much to pay you with.' My voice must've sounded so desperate, the guy took pity on me, but I think it was more to do with the fact that he was afraid of me. He took the meat, wrapped it in brown paper, and handed it to me. I noticed his hand shook with nerves as he did so and yet resisted the temptation to ask what I really was. Although I had a suspicion, he already knew.

'Here, take it, I shouldn't, but oh go on...it would've gone for dog scraps anyway.'
I nodded in thanks and tucked the meat under my jacket. As I left the shop, I could sense he was still looking at me from the window. Without realising it, he had saved me from going back to my old habits. Unless that was his intention in the beginning.

The ship horn blared almost startling me. I took another bite of the meat from the brown wrapper and stood behind the wire fence watching the ships being unloaded. I covered my eyes as the glare from the midday sun beamed down sending a dull ache to the back of my head. Now I had to find a way on one of these things. I took my sleeve and wiped the blood from my mouth. Damn, I thought, looking at my jacket. I was in dire need for new clothes, but right now, that was the least of my worries. Somehow and for whatever reason, I had a feeling I had get to New York right away, even though there was no rational explanation for it. The name just entered my stream of thoughts and besides, after reading the book I had found at the house I just had a feeling it was the right thing to do.

'Are you supposed to be 'ere doll?'
I froze.

I reveled in the sweetness of her voice for a split second before I turned my head towards her, trying desperately not to make eye contact. I didn't want to alarm her.

'I, er...was just wondering when the ship was due to leave?'
Fuck, I hope my voice didn't sound too threatening.

From the corner of my eye, I noticed she placed her hands on her hips and shook her head at me curiously. 'You're not one of those ship spotters are you? Oh well, I'll check the timetable for you,' she said, as she walked back into her office.

'1.15 am love,' she shouted out.
I nodded in thanks but just as I was about to walk away, I heard a revving of a motorcycle behind me.

CHAPTER FOUR

The ship wasn't due to leave until the morning, so I had some time to stave off until then. As night-time approached I left the docks to walk back into Helsinki city. Hunger was calling and the only place I knew where I could find some food was from the butcher shop. I wasn't so concerned about the motorcyclist; I guess if he wanted to harm me, he would've done it when he had the chance. Although, it did occur to me, who is much stronger than I am anyway. After all, I was a vampire, so why should I have to fear. It was quite a chilly night too, so I put my hands in my jacket pocket and kept my head down. After walking for twenty minutes I found myself at the harbour. I inhaled the fresh air and relaxed in the gentle sound of the sea, which always brought out the melancholy side in me. Soon my peace was shattered by the cry of a woman's voice.

'Vampyri!'

'What?' I mumbled to myself. Did I hear right? The mere mention of vampyri was enough to stop me in my tracks, but surely it wasn't aimed at me. Was it? This country was seeped in folklore, my folklore. I lifted my head and looked around the harbour. Aside from the fluttering of the sails in the breeze, it was desolate of people, which added an eerie resonance to it tonight.

'Vampyri?'

I heard her voice again, calling from the direction of the boats. I couldn't see anyone at first but soon appeared a middle aged woman. Her long blonde hair gently swished in the breeze as she stood at the hull of her boat. She pointed a finger towards me and called out again.

'Vampyri. Yes, you, I know what you are.'

My eyes widened at her revelation.

As I walked towards her brimming with curiosity, her voice became even louder.

'No, you stay there, don't you dare come any closer. You should leave and never come back here; your kind is not welcome.'

'How do you know what I am?'

'It's the gypsy trait in me. Inherited from my grandmother who was savaged to death on the islands many years ago. My grandfather swore it was a demon that had killed her, but the authorities laughed at him, said he was a fool for believing in such things.'

This cannot be happening to me.

I felt panicked by her revelation. 'I didn't kill her,' I yelled back. I was certain I didn't.

'But one of your kind did. Now go, you are not welcome here.'

I was about to walk away when she called me back.

'Oh one more thing...the one thing you really want, will be yours but there will be a price to pay.'

What could I say? She was scaring me on the quiet. I didn't want to bother her no more so I quickly turned away and walked into the city centre. I was shocked and as if my mind didn't have enough to contend with, I was now left with worrying over what she meant by her words.

I kept my head down, trying not to draw any more attention to myself. As I turned the street corner, I was greeted by the sound of life and laughter that resonated from every bar and club along the main street. Loneliness soon crept back like the plague as I watched the show of human affection around me. I was doing my best to remain calm in such an awkward predicament, but the blood was just lingering in the air, teasing me. I knew I had to find the butchers again and fast if I was not going to feast on these humans tonight. I kept thinking about the meat I had earlier, hoping it would keep my mind off the scantily dressed women lingering by the doorway of the bar. They were looking at me and smiling. I guess they were too drunk to use their common sense. Nervously I pushed my hair back from my face and returned the sentient. Should I have done that? I freaked out. I was still prising myself off human blood and stupidly without thinking I was making gestures towards these women. What in the hell was I doing. As I walked past I could hear the women jeer as their friend, a tall brunette in a tight fitted red dress came stumbling over towards me.

'Go on, give him a kiss,' they shouted, encouraging her on in a drunken stupor.

I avoided any eye contact and kept walking, secretly hoping she would go away, but she didn't. I kept walking faster as I knew it could be fatal if she tried, well I presumed it would be, as I've never been kissed before to really know. My hunger was also reaching a danger point, so when I heard the incessant tapping of her heels behind me, I quickened up my pace a bit more. The next thing I knew she grabbed my arm and pulled me towards her body. Her soft wet lips, that tasted of berry lipgloss pressed firmly onto mine. I was too weak to fight her off me.

'What are you doing? Get away from him you stupid bitch,' I heard a man yell.

I opened my eyes and pushed the woman away from me. The last thing I wanted was any trouble, especially now that I was hungry and could feel myself shifting at any given moment.

'Hey! You! Stay away from the women, you fucking freak, yeah that's right, a freak!' he kept yelling at me.

Something snapped within me. I just stood and glared at him like a hunter. He was much stockier and bigger built than myself, but I knew I had the strength of ten compared to him. He pushed my shoulder, trying to get a reaction from me. 'Don't push me; step away now and no-one will get hurt,' I glowered

He started pushing me again and laughing at me in a mocking tone. 'Oh listen to this freak guys, he reckons he can fight me.'

'Leave me alone, you do not want to piss me off I can assure you!' I snarled under my breath.

'Let him go, please. He's not worth it,' the woman begged him.

'So he can go and try it on with some other woman? He's not natural, there's something not quite right about him.'

'He's different, now just let him go will you,' the brunette shouted.

'You got that right, honey. He's a freak of nature.'

He kept going on and on and his voice was drowning out my thoughts and interrupting my concentration. I couldn't shake off the urge to bite. A few of his friends came running over. I felt panicky as the overwhelming feeling of fear enclosed me, trapping me like a wretched animal. 'Attack Jyrki, attack,' I heard a snide voice inside my head. It wasn't mine. Why am I allowing them to make me feel like this? The conflicting argument continued its battle; it was either the demon or walk away. I was hungry though and my throat yearned for her blood.

'Arghh!' I yelled as I felt a thump at the back of my neck. I fell forwards on all fours, reeling with rage and anger. I felt another kick on my side and the sound of insane laughter around me.

I braced myself, and looked up towards the women who were now screaming and backing away. My gaze now fixed on the man with the sarcastic smile and stupid arrogance that he could even win a fight with me. I smirked at him, fully aware my eyes hinted a shade of yellow and my fangs had now perfectly cut through.

'Didn't your mother ever tell you never to pick a fight with a vampire?' I laughed as I watched the colour drain from his chubby face.

I leapt from the floor and grabbed him around the neck. He was shaking as I sniffed the blood that emanated from him his flesh.

'What the fuck are you?' he croaked.

'I'm your worst bloody nightmare.'

His friends, hardly believing I had the strength in me backed away. Although, I was sure they saw my face shift by the screams of the women huddled together by bar door.

'Just let him go mister,' the woman called out to me. 'We don't want any trouble.'

I didn't want to. I pressed the tip of my tooth onto the flesh and slowly made a puncture. The guy whimpered and I could smell the sweat and fear emanating from him. Still, I was perfectly aware I had an audience and so licked the tiny speck of blood that dripped from the wound and with all my strength pushed him away from me.

I stood for a little while watching the terrified human shake and wither in agony on the floor. He held his hand firmly onto the wound and sat staring at me with a horrified look on his face. As his friends helped him up from the floor, they all turned to me with vacant expressions on their faces. They said nothing to me; I could sense they were too scared to do so.

'What the fuck did I do that for?' I ran at an alarming speed through the town. I ran until it pained me, allowing my feet to take me anywhere. I ended up standing in the middle of the Senate Square feeling disorientated as I clasped my eyes on the neo-classical buildings that surrounded me.

My concentration was shattered, my strength whittled to nothing. I had almost killed another human tonight and the worst thing was there were witnesses. I could feel a tear running down my face as I walked towards the statue in the centre. I sat myself down and rested my back against the cold structure. It wasn't so much different to me.

Yet I felt assured in the knowledge I could resist the blood if I so badly wanted to. It was a small comfort to wrap my head around on this cold night. I hoped the morning would bring a new beginning to this disastrous end. New York was beckoning me.

CHAPTER FIVE

'Alright mate, got any spare change have yer?'

I wasn't in the mood for this. Two weeks spent in a cramped cargo ship and I was as pissed off as anything.

'Do I look like I have any?' I spat.

I must've jerked my head around so sharply I saw the homeless guy almost fall off the kerb.

'Jesus boy, you are one scary piece of shit,' he shouted as I watched him run down the road to his mate.

'Do I really look so bad? Must've been the glare,' I chuckled to myself as I turned to walk away. Worriedly, I stopped and glanced at my reflection in a shop window. No wonder the guy had run off. I could see my somewhat 35 year old appearance had taken quite a beating being cooped up for the past fortnight. If that wasn't all, my fangs were still in place from when I had the last drop of blood back in Helsinki. 'Damn,' I cussed as I cast my eye over my slender statuesque frame. My leather jacket looked as if it was about to disintegrate off me. Draven had found it on one of his nights out and gave it to me, as it didn't fit him. He was forever dodging the safe zone without father knowing. It looked like I was in need of a cleanup not to scare away any more New Yorkers.

As I walked into one of the biggest cities in the world, my nerves began to take a toll on me. I began to wonder what in the hell possessed me to come here in the first place. I hoped I'd be harder to track in such a vast area but I felt slightly uneasy. As if I was being watched.

My eyes looked around in wonderment at the stone cold gargoyle like state it was. As I marveled at the bustling of crowds that surrounded me, it dawned on me that these people weren't really living in this suppressed place. The flashing of the neon lights set against the grey backdrop that came at me from all angles, proved to me how uncultured and plastic the 21st century had become. This was very different from the serene, untouched beauty of my homeland deep within the Finnish forests.

I placed my hands in my jacket pockets and just stood there gazing up at the skyscrapers for a while. I was in awe.

Standing on the edge of the sidewalk just off Broadway, I inhaled the smell of blood that encroached me from all directions. To my ancestors this would have been a playground in their lust for blood, but for me now, I was quite content with my regular top ups at the butchers.

It was a warm day. I was aware I was receiving odd glances from people as I walked passed them. People sensed there was something different about me, but I was cool with that, I had no desire to drain them.

I walked idly along the sidewalk, looking up now and then at the people passing by. I was aware they were snatching a quick glimpse of me. In fact I was getting a kick out of their curiosity. Although by now, the sun was now making me feel quite tetchy and irritable and it wasn't such a good idea to be hanging around a major city like this. That's when I noticed some sunglasses on display outside a shop. I bit my lip and did a quick scan around me. No one was remotely interested, so I sidled up to the stand and snatched a pair of silver aviator glasses that I fancied. I felt the theft was justified. My eyes ached and I didn't want to get cranky with so many humans around.

'Mom?'
I heard the voice call. Startled, I turned around and saw a small boy, no older than five standing next to his mother by the hot dog cart.

'Is that man a vampire?'

'What man?' she asked in a broad New York accent.

'That man,' the child pointed towards me.
'What the hell,' I panicked. I looked away quickly to avoid any more unwanted attention. I picked up the newspaper on the stand and began to flick through it, trying my hardest to look invisible.
The mother knelt down beside the child and whispered, 'That's not a nice thing to say,' while glaring up at me.

'But Mom, he is.'

'Just stop it, ok, it's so rude of you,' she huffed
I peered over the newspaper and flashed the child a snide grin. 'Shush,' I said as I placed my finger over my lips. The child's eyes widened and stood open mouthed. He tugged his mother's coat again and began to cry.

'Y'know, you've got to quit reading them comic books,' the mother said infuriatingly as she grabbed the child's arm and stormed across the road.

It was truly fascinating to watch a child so boldly admit who I was. I folded the newspaper and put it back. Pushed my glasses up to the bridge of nose and walked across the crossing.

'I'm the walking myth the ordinary people fear, and they don't even know it,' I remarked to myself as I watched them mingle in amongst the crowd.

My mood lifted a bit after that. I spent the rest of the day walking around with a childlike fascination at the world. Yet the loneliness was something I don't think I could never get used to.

'Dracula?'

I ripped the poster from the wall outside the cinema and stood looking at the slightly exaggerated impression these humans had of vampires. I grinned to myself and shook my head in disbelief. If only he were still alive, I would've had a friend to talk to all these years. Just as I was about to throw the crumpled poster I heard the revving of a motorcycle again. 'How odd, that's the same bike I saw in Finland?'

I pushed my glasses back up onto the bridge of my nose again and carried on walking. Every now and then, I'd glance behind me for the bike.

'Something isn't right'' I slipped my hand between the buttons on my shirt, checking if the Ankh was still there, until I realised if it wasn't I wouldn't be here now. 'Paranoia,' I thought that was something only humans got. The whole city felt like it was closing in on me. Desperate to get out of the busiest part of the city I walked and walked until I found myself in the backstreets. Although it didn't take too long for somebody to notice me again.

'Yo mister!'

'Oh crap, what now?' I was feeling a little tetchy and hungry. I glared over to the street opposite. There was a bunch of youngsters sitting on the steps of a derelict building, looking over at me curiously.

'What's up?' My accent was deeply strange and foreign, which probably only enticed their curiosity even more.

I stood waiting on the opposite side for a response. I clenched my fists tightly thinking they were going to start a fight, when suddenly the guy with the green mohican got up and walked over. Tension mounted. My body felt like I was shifting. I growled lightly under my breath. Just

30

when I thought things were going to get ugly, the guy handed me a leaflet.

'You look like the kind of guy that might be interested in this,' he said.

I took the leaflet from his hands. He stood there perplexed, as if he hasn't seen a foreigner before.

'Yeah, um...' Was all he could say. I sensed there must've been a billion things in his head right now but unlike a child he wouldn't admit to calling me a vampire.

I decided to put him out of his misery.

'I'm Finnish.'

'Oh that's it then...well, come to the Zone tonight dude. It's a new club, plus we have The Ramones playing a one off gig...' he said backing away from me.

'The Ramones?'

'It's a band...y'know, music?' he laughed nervously.

He looked at me as if I had fallen from mars, but I knew what music was. I heard it on my jaunts out in Helsinki.

'Sure, I'll be there.'

Finally, now I have some connection with this crazy world.

'So where's the best place to hang around here?'

'In the Bronx? You gotta be kidding right,' he shouted over as I watched him walk back to his mates.

I stuffed the leaflet in my pocket and continued to walk idly around the corner.

'That bloody motorcycle again.' This time the mysterious driver lifted up his visor and looked at me before speeding off.

I had a sinking feeling this had something to do with the prophecy.

CHAPTER SIX

'Get a job, you bum!'

I glanced up at the young man in the pinstripe suit and briefcase who had the audacity to make those assumptions about me. I pulled my sunglasses down and shot him a glare with my eyes. They had a tendency to shift from ice blue to a hint of yellow when I was angry. It always seemed to freak people out. And I was right; he flinched and couldn't walk past quick enough. I sniggered to myself as I watched the office workers rush past on their way home. At least they had the sense to stay away from me.

It was almost dusk and the city was beginning to show its true colours. The darkness always brought out the worst in places, which I knew very well. For a while, I sat on the steps of the cathedral wondering what my next move should be. The motorcyclist hadn't shown up for hours. Therefore, I had time to conceive a plan of action if things went awry.

Yet, like always I found my mind wandering and my thoughts quickly turned to the prophecy. Father had relied on me to return the Ankh to Egypt. I never fully understood why, I guess there were some things he just couldn't talk about. All I knew was it had to be returned one day to save our souls, as he used to tell me, but with The Others lurking, God knows where, I knew I had to keep the Ankh out of sight before they end up on my trail again. Besides, what would happen to me if I returned it? That wasn't something I wanted to think about right now.

For now, at least, I wanted a taste of living; even though I knew I was half dead. Suddenly a few specks of rain tapped me on my shoulder as if demanding me to get a move on.

I put my hands in my jacket pocket and pulled out the flyer I got earlier. I un-crumpled the paper and read the advert. Why not, I thought, at least I would be dry, and it's not like I have anywhere to go tonight.

The humans were almost becoming second nature to me anyway, when it dawned on me, I hadn't ate a single thing all day. 'Damn I'd better get something to eat. Just to be on the safe side,' I mumbled to myself. I stuffed the flyer back in my pocket and got up in search of the food I was promised by the butcher. He said he would leave it outside the back entrance of the shop after closing.

It was pitch black apart from the flickering of the lamp in the lane. And unnervingly quiet. I could smell the blood from the scraps of meat a few yards away. Thankfully, my sense of smell leaned more towards the animal rather than human these days. Of course, I didn't want to analyse it, as part of me was glad this has happened. Yet the other half of me, the non-demonic part, didn't want to crave blood at all.

It wasn't fun to be a vampire these days, especially with my recent discovery that the media had gone into a frenzy over us. I had such a shock when I arrived in New York and saw all the commercial crap for the vampire films and books that were out. If only we could descend back into the shadows again and become the princes of darkness that we truly are, I thought as I sat laughing to myself. Ah well, I'd better make the most of it here, maybe Hollywood would come knocking on my door one day.

I took the meat from the cardboard box the butcher had kindly left and sunk my teeth into it. I hadn't fully realised how hungry I was. Feeling satisfied I wiped my mouth of the excess blood and broke down.

This was becoming repetitive. The meat seeking, blood craving, demon dodging was a curse I wanted to be shot of. As I sat back against the brick wall, feeling somewhat sorry for myself, I happened to look up and notice the flicker of the street lamp become more erratic.

A frown drew across my face. Without any warning, the sound of a revving motorbike came closer and closer. I sensed I was in danger, so I leapt to my feet and snarled. I could feel the vampire surging through my body. With my teeth clenched and my fists ready, I knew I could take on whoever dared cross my path. The bike was now heading towards me almost blinding me with its headlight. As it swerved in front me, blocking me up against the wall, I suddenly felt ready to release the demon. Not that I wanted to shift. I felt I had no choice but to defend myself. I stood my ground as I could now feel myself shifting completely into vampire mode.

The fangs began to descend from the gum and my eyes became lucid. My head tilted back as the pain shot through my spine. I hadn't shifted for so long I had forgotten how it felt.

'Nooo! Don't fuckin' do that,' the voice boomed from the helmet.

I inhaled. It was human blood. This had to be a trap. I tried desperately to stop the transformation, as I knew I was far more dangerous when I was complete. I sank to the floor on all fours withering in agony, as my whole body allowed the demon to come through. It was no wonder Father had taken us to Scandinavia away from the humans. Who in the world wanted to live like this?

Wait a minute. I know that accent. It reminded me of the guy outside the house in Finland.

Now I was confused. I controlled my breathing and relaxed a bit, hoping the shifting would somehow stop. I looked up at the figure in black leather that sat on the motorcycle waving its arms about like a lunatic.

'Don't fucking shift completely; you will be in so much danger. Just try to control it.'

He knows about the vampire. 'You've been following me since Helsinki. Who the fuck are you?' I seethed

I kept a watchful eye on him as he removed his helmet.

'I'm Stride. It's nice to finally meet ya Jyrki.'

'What? I know you too,' I said bewilderedly. He pulled his long grey hair out of his ponytail and loosened his scarf a bit.

'That's bloody better. Yeah, I know you Jyrki, so you can calm down now. I'm not going to bloody hurt ya, as if I could anyway.'

'So h-h-how do you know who I am? You're not one of...those are you?'

He smiled and began to remove his leather gloves before stuffing them in his jacket pocket.

'Hey, do I look like a fucking demon?'

I laughed nervously. He probably wasn't aware demons could look like a regular person.

'Maybe it's best if I explain things somewhere else. Hop on the back.' he said, passing me a helmet.

I was hesitant.

'Look, you are more of a danger to me, ok?'

Of course, I had to agree with him. Now that I was stood next to him, I sniffed. He seemed very much human.

'Now get rid of those fangs alright and no nipping me on the neck.'

For a human, he didn't seem too bad. I had my reservations of course, but I picked up some good vibes off him. Also, he wasn't so easily freaked out when he saw me change whereas any other human would've.

'So, er, where's the accent from?'

'Scotland. Can you understand me alright? A lot of folk around here have trouble with it.'

'Yeah, I understand you perfectly. It's just that I'm sure I've heard it somewhere before that's all.'

I caught him smiling as he put his helmet back on.

'Anywhere particular?' he shouted over the noise of the revving engine.

'Let's go to the Zone club. It was where I was headed to anyway,' I shouted

'Right you are boss.'

CHAPTER SEVEN

Stride rode the motorcycle like maniac. Between getting soaked and windswept, I somehow felt a bout of nausea as the passing of the neon lights on either side of my head was making me disoriented. At least when I run, I thought, it is more like a fleeting sensation of being here one minute and there the next. I couldn't wait until he parked up. I was beginning to have visions of the Exorcist scene in my head. Please I begged, don't let me do it.

Finally, I could see the venue on the right hand side of the road. Nerves began telling on me as I saw the long queue of people waiting outside. I just hoped the last bit of food I had would last me.

'Stride, take the next turning,' I yelled, tapping him on the shoulder.

'No problem, so ya like The Ramones then?' he hollered in his thick Scottish accent.

'Excuse me?'

'The bloody band we've come here to see?' he laughed

'Oh, I've never heard of them until today.'

'You what?' he laughed at me again, 'then what have you been doing all these years, hiding in the woods?'

'You're not far off,' I shrugged. What have I been doing all these years though?

He took the next right turning and parked up opposite the venue. I was so relieved to get off the damn thing.

'Now, which pocket did I put it in?' he said to himself

I watched him as he prattled about with the numerous pockets that he had on his black biker jacket.

'What are you doing?' I asked, looking at him curiously.

'Oh! Don't mind these,' he said as he pulled out a wooden stake and a knife before throwing them into his bag.

'They were just for precaution that's all,' he assured me with a smile.

'I certainly hope so. So who are you then? And what do you want with me?'

His smile disappeared and a look of concern drew across his face, which alarmed me greatly. I had every reason not to trust him. I decided to give him the benefit of the doubt. If he was working with the

Others, then I'd kill him. That was my plan, actually it was the only plan I had right now.

'I'll explain what I can in here rather than outside, the music will drown out our conversation. You never know who's listening in these days.'

I nodded in agreement. I looked at him with his head of long white hair and his American Indian beads dangling from his neck onto his plain black t-shirt. He was by far the most eccentric human I ever come across.

'So, are you ready then? I'm quite looking forward to this, I haven't seen a good band since...oh Black Sabbath in the 70's, and that was in Glasgow. What a night that was. Remember me to tell you about it sometime,' he said.

I had a feeling this was going to be a long night.

It was still raining. I took one look at the queue and thought fuck it. The door was manned by two huge guys. They didn't faze me at all.

'Hey Stride, follow me.'

We walked past the long line of people standing beside the wall of the venue. As I passed, I could sense the women were staring at me and giggling. I returned the favour and smiled back at them, almost sending them into a frenzy. I knew women found us vampires far more attractive than the average man, but usually once they get too close their lust often turned to fear. I glanced over my shoulder and saw Stride flashing them a wink, when I realised they were laughing and mocking him behind his back. Poor guy, I smirked. I don't think I had this much fun in years.

'How the fuck did you do that?' he said obviously catching on to his failed attempt at wooing the opposite sex.

'Luck,' I shrugged.

'So how are we supposed to get past those two Rottweiler's then - luck too?' he said, pointing at the security by the door.

'C'mon...we can get in, no problem. Just watch.'

I only had to look at the guy.

'Alright mate...er, Mick.' I said reading his security pass. 'We can go through ok?' I said quite confidently to him. I half expected him to throw me onto the kerb, but he just stood by the door with his arms folded. Stride edged away slightly. The doorman looked me up and down again with a curious frown on his face. After a few seconds of deliberating, he nodded his head.

'Go on, go through.'

'How did you do tha'?'

'One of the advantages of being a Vampire,' I remarked. Either that or they thought I was a member of the band.'

Stride laughed.

'Jesus, it fucking stinks in 'ere.'

I nodded in agreement. The stench of stale beer and piss was even making me wince. We walked up the staircase to the bar, dodging the youngsters sat on the steps drinking and smoking. A couple looked at me inquisitively then carried on sucking each other's faces off.

'Get us a pint will ya? Oh and here's some cash, as I know you ain't got any.'

He thrust a ten-dollar bill into my hand and went to find a table at the back of the room. 'A pint?' I muttered looking at the strange piece of paper he pressed into my hand. I had read about currency in a book back at the old farmhouse, but I had never seen it with my own eyes before.

'Hey, move it fella,' some guy shouted as he walked past me.

I realised I was standing in the way of the incoming crowd from the door as I could hear the snide remarks of the youngsters as they brushed passed me. I walked over to the bar, not sure of what to ask for when I caught sight of the women dressed in fishnet and patent leather miniskirts dancing seductively around a pole on the stage. A smug look drew across my face. The intense beat of the industrial sound pounded against my chest, almost as if I had a heartbeat. I felt like I belonged here, another reject of modern society.

'What are you having?' I heard the barmaid call.

I edged closer to the bar and smiled at her. She leaned over, knowing very well her bust almost bulged over her red corset. Not that I minded but I could see the lust in her eyes as she looked me over. She flicked her long dark hair over her shoulder and fluttered her obviously fake dark lashes at me. I averted my gaze to the ten dollar bill Stride gave me to calm my nerves.

'Umm...' What was I supposed to say, I didn't know of any alcoholic drinks. Feeling stupid, I turned to the guy sat next to me.

38

'Whatever he's drinking,' I said to her.

'Then it's two beers okay sweets.'

The moment was becoming a little too intense. She never took her gaze off me as she slid her hand over mine before taking the note. I felt a slight shiver up my spine as I felt the warm touch of human flesh against mine. I was sorely tempted.

'It could've been blood for all you know,' I heard the guy next to me say.

Feeling more at ease I turned sideways to make conversation. The guy was knelt over the bar sipping on his drink. His long black hair draped over the shoulders of his leather jacket. I was so glad of the interruption.

'Then that would've been perfect,' I replied

If only you knew, if only you knew.

'Hey, I'm Blaze by the way,' he said holding his hand out in a gesture.

'I'm Jyrki.'

'That accent isn't American?' he asked

'No, I'm Finnish...'

Just as I was about to say something else I heard Stride hollering from across the room.

'Where are the drinks?'

'Bloody Stride,' I muttered.

The barmaid put the drinks on a tray and smiled at me seductively before serving the next customer. I held the tray up with the beers hoping it would shut him up.

Blaze sniggered.

'It looks like your old man is thirsty.'

'He isn't my old man, thank fuck,' I said as I left the bar.

I walked over to the table, careful not to spill my drinks on anyone. The place began to fill up quite quickly and I almost had to wedge myself between the tables.

'Take a seat...' Stride pointed out a chair and took his pint off the tray before I had a chance to sit down.

I sat waiting until he had a sufficient amount of drink to satisfy his thirst. Slowly he placed the half drank glass on the table and looked at me. He leaned over the table and in a whisper, he muttered in my ear.

'I know you are a New Blood,' he said as he sat back and folded his arms.

I sighed deeply, never have I heard that word spoken by a human before. For a few moments, I just sat here and tapped my fingers on the table. 'What do you know?' I said leaning towards him

'Well, my name is Stride, and before you ask it's not my real name it's a name that was given to me by my biker buddies, and yes, I am a vampire watcher. I've called myself that for the past 40 years,' he said picking up his drink, 'ever since my Father…oh nevermind that now.'

'So what am I supposed to do... congratulate you? I said back with a hint of sarcasm. 'What do you know of the New Bloods? Did someone send you?'

'Nobody sent me as such. It's a bit of a long story right now, I will tell you again, but first thing first, the important bit, you ought to be careful now as by coming here the prophecy has now taken into effect. I am aware of a secret order that have been sent out to hunt you down...'

'Hunt me?'

'Yes Jyrki, they want the Ankh. Y'see I've been following you to make sure you don't get yourself into any bother. Call me a guardian or whatever, but even you should know how destructive that Ankh could be if it got into the wrong hands.'

'Who is the Secret Order? And do they know I'm here yet?'

'You know how you descended from Egypt right? And that your race was a mistake and Ramesses wanted nothing to do with the vampires? Well, after your father took the Ankh from Egypt for safety during the blood war, an aide to Ramesses, called Jafar, was ordered to ensure the vampires would be wiped from Egyptian history, but, and this is a big but, he was nothing more than a two faced power freak that has been searching for you for centuries. He wants something you have. That silver Ankh you have tucked behind your t shirt.'

'Wouldn't that would make him an immortal?'

'Yes. He used the same ancient spell from the Book of the Dead, but he's not a vampire, not like you. Hell, we're not even sure what he is. Now he is after the second part of the prophecy, which has been hidden since modern civilisation began. We're not even sure if it exists, to be honest. We had a tip off it's in the Book of The Dead but at the moment we can't get access to it, not even for a little look.'

'And he wants that for what?'
'To find you, find out how you will defeat him, it's all in there.'

CHAPTER EIGHT

The post punk anarchistic sound pounded from the amps. I sipped on my drink, which I was duly informed at the bar it was in fact called beer. Well, whatever it was I needed it right now. The odd taste didn't bode too well with my palate either. I winced as I swallowed the vile stuff.

'Not to your liking then?' he said, with a sarcastic tone.

'It'll grow on me I'm sure,' I said, not really convinced as I put the bottle back on the table.

I leaned back in my chair letting everything he had just told me unscramble in my head. Of course I knew about my history but I guess I didn't quite know it all. Stride was very on edge as I had noticed that in the twenty minutes we had been here he had not once really met my gaze. His eyes flickered around the room, watching people as if they were suspects.

'So this Jafar is in New York right now?'

It took him a few seconds to answer as he took a puff on the cigarette he had just lit.

'I'm not a hundred per cent certain, but the uncanny thing is, the Book of The Dead is on loan at the New York museum now for some exhibit called, er, The Egyptian's and The Afterlife, or something.'

'Is it really? So, the first part of the prophecy, where is that?'

Stride shifted about uncomfortably in his chair. I figured he knew where it was, but seemed reluctant to tell me.

'It's safe. Don't worry about that now. Let's just concentrate on getting the second part okay? Or we'll never know how this story is going to end. Just promise me you will keep the Ankh out of sight, ok. They won't be after you in daylight as I have a hunch they will bide their time with this. It's just a matter of keeping yourself to yourself for now, alright?'

'What do they want with the Ankh anyway? What are they planning on doing?'

'They're trying to get the Ankh for their own selfish needs. It holds the power of the Ancient Gods doesn't it? Only someone with a pure heart can use it you see, someone who has a special path in life, but I'm sure they would find a way of manipulating it. I had heard about an apocalypse, but I can't be certain on those facts right now either. The twist to the tale is, you haven't been allowed to return it yet because written in the prophecy is your name, as the one who will avenge them. So now we've established someone is after it, now guess why they want it?'

I was almost too scared to say it. I picked up the bottle of beer and downed the last drop. 'To create more vampires...I wonder if it's the Others?'

'Others?' Stride frowned at me and shook his head. 'I don't know about them, but you've got it in one mate, and that's why I've been called. We've been searching for you since we found some information leading to your whereabouts. Now listen, stay out of sight and for fuck sake, try and act a little...human.'

'You know that's not going to be easy...hey, so it was you I saw in Finland?'

'Of course, I wanted to get to you first before they did. I owed it to someone,' he winked

I hadn't even begun to question him when he gulped down the remainder of his drink and rested his hand on my shoulder.

'Don't look for me, I know when and if I need to find you, ok?' he said, taking his leather jacket off the back of the chair. I watched him walk towards the exit until he disappeared in amongst the crowd. Now what was I meant to do. I sat alone at the table mulling over what I should do next. Night-time I was at my most vulnerable and I was slowly getting drunk, so I had no choice but to stay low in this place for a while. Still, I was so pissed I had not known about the Secret Order or whoever the fuck they were. Also, he was still a bit of a mystery too. My head was all over the place and it wasn't because of the drink.

'Hey!'

I heard the voice shout from across the table. I glanced up from my drink and saw a familiar face from earlier.

'Ah! Blaze right?' My voice began to slur and I was only on my first bottle.

'Mind if I join you?' he asked, handing me another drink.

'Sure, why not, just as long as you're not a vampire hunter.' I laughed.
'Eh?' he said.

'Oh I'm sorry, bad joke. You're better off paying no attention to anything I say. I don't usually drink this stuff,' I slurred.

'I can't say I'm surprised to hear that considering you didn't know what you were ordering at the bar earlier,' he sniggered. 'And you had Raven the waitress lusting after you. Do you know I've been trying to get a date with her for two months and you walk in here and she's putty in your hands,' he smiled.

My instinct told me immediately he was a good guy. I had no desire to drink his blood either, which was also good thing. Maybe being intoxicated was the way to go. Numbs out even the worst in vampires.

'Er, yeah I did notice the obvious, but um, she's not really my type,' I said.

Blaze raised one of his dark eyebrows and scoffed. 'You are fucking joking right. She's hot,' he said pointing towards her at the bar.

I turned around to see her talking to a few other females sipping their drinks by the bar. One woman in particular did catch my attention.

'Do you sing by any chance?'

'Sing? Man, I don't think I could hold a fucking tune right now,' I hollered above the music which just so happened had been cranked up a few decibels.

'I see you can't hold your drink,' he laughed

'Tell me about it. My head is bloody spinning here,' I said, picking up the other bottle.

'Not often we get new faces in here. What it is my band, The Black Stones have been offered a few gigs with a chance of getting signed but our singer quit on us a month ago...'

'Me? Sing? Umm, I got a lot on right now...'

'Sure, I bet you could pull in the ladies no problem though?'

'Yeah, about that...I don't know if it's such a good idea,' I said with a smirk.

Curiosity was sure getting the best of him. He was about to ask me something when this pretty woman from the bar tapped him on the shoulder.

I noticed her green eyes latch on me instantly as she bent down to whisper in Blaze's ear. Suddenly my chest began to feel a little tense as

I smiled back at her. Simply beautiful, I thought. She was the most pleasing thing to my eye in a long time.

'Erm, Jyrki? This is my sister April...April this is Jyrki.'

She swept her long dark hair off her shoulders and reached out her delicate hand in a gesture. No woman has ever looked at me with such warmth before. Usually they were so transfixed by my looks or running away scared.

'It's a pleasure to meet you.'

'Wow that accent is awesome. Where are you from?'

She nudged Blaze to move up and sat down on the chair opposite me.

I was feeling a little nervous and for the first time that I was aware of I was actually overcome with shyness. My bottle of beer instantly became a firm friend as I took another swig to calm my nerves.

'Well I'm originally from Finland.'

'Yeah? Well your English is great, where did you learn it?'

'I'm a fast learner.'

She smiled. 'So what are you doing here then?'

Bloody hell, I thought. She can half talk.

'I just felt like a break.' That was all I could think of to say to her right now. I picked up my drink and took another swig of the bottle. Right now, I was well and truly intoxicated.

'Hey sis, leave the guy alone alone ok,' he said with a laugh. 'I got to him first. He's thinking of joining The Black Stones, aren't you?'

I hoped he was joking.

April laughed. 'You're joining these guys? You must be crazy.'

I grinned, still unable to take my eyes off her. It felt so good to be in such good company for a change.

'We're heading back to my flat after the gig for a party. You're more than welcome to come?' Blaze asked.

Should I. Usually humans were lunch to my people.

CHAPTER NINE

It was early hours in the next morning when we decided to leave the club. Blaze was feeling a touch sober and so offered me a lift back to his place in his van. I was feeling reluctant to as the blood I had earlier was slightly wearing off. I didn't want to crave the blood of someone I've just befriended. So while Blaze went over to the bar to speak with the waitress I decided to leave.

  I was hoping I'd go unnoticed but as I walked across the sticky, beer stained dance floor towards the exit, I saw April come out of the ladies room.

Just keep on walking.

  'Hi, so you're leaving then?'

I halted. Part of me couldn't bear to ignore her.

  The rock music slowed down to a softer tempo and I heard the waitress call in the last orders of the night. Did I really want to leave right now? It was decision time.

  I towered over her, casting my eyes down her petite frame towards her skin-tight leather trousers. She gazed up at me; her eyeliner smudged around the contour of her deep-set green eyes. I felt a tugging feeling in the pit of my stomach and the urge for blood. I wanted her blood.

  This was far too dangerous.

Still transfixed by her smile, I extended my hand and tried to string a coherent sentence together.

  'Umm, It's best if I do leave, but it's been an absolute pleasure to have met you and Blaze though.'

She brushed a strand of hair over her ears and nodded quite sadly.

'Well, likewise, but you'll be back here next time, right?'

  I averted my gaze from her pleading eyes and shook my head. 'No, I don't think so.' As much I wanted too, it was not a good idea. The music stopped and my eyes veered towards her one more time. 'I must go.'

  I thought it was strange how she showed no fear.

I followed the crowd toward the exit and pushed my way to the bottom of the stairs. As I stepped out of the door, I heard…

  'Jyrki! Where the fuck are you going? My van is up this way.'

Fuck. It's Blaze.

I intended to walk away but as I stood in the cold, wet rain; looking up at the street ahead I saw a very bleak future waiting for me. My instinct told me to turn around. It had been right so far, so that's what I did.

'April said she saw you leaving. So are you coming to the party or what?'

'Could you drop me down to the docks first?' I asked. I remembered when I got off the ship that there was a slaughterhouse just across the way. My throat was dry and I needed more blood, as I could not afford to get tetchy around these humans. Blaze did not seem to want to ask me why; he just nodded and opened the van door for me. I found him to be quite a carefree and easygoing character. Before he started the engine, I watched him with curiosity as he tied his long dark hair back and put on his sunglasses. He noticed I was looking at him peculiarly and laughed.

'It's Rock 'n Roll man...'

'Sunglasses at night?' I said to him. I should've thought of this before. 'So, is April coming?' I asked sheepishly.

'Er, no mate, we'll see her later I hope. She had a call from work she did, so she took off about two minutes ago. I've no idea what for at this time of the morning. So, did you enjoy the pre-Halloween gig then? The Ramones were fucking awesome weren't they?'

'Well, to be honest it was all new to me, but I thought they were great. I reckon it'd be awesome to play like them.'

Well, it had to be better than my life anyhow.

Blaze looked at me and smiled. 'That's good to hear because we're playing in there for Halloween in a week.'

'Halloween?'

'Yeah, you know, the night of the dead?'

I laughed. 'I most certainly do.'

'Ok, here we go, not going to be too long are you?' he said, pulling up by the entrance gates.

'No, I won't be a moment, just have something to do.'

'Okay, no probs. I'll just let the guys know I'll be a bit late,' he said looking at a small strange box.

I stood against the wall of the entrance where I could see the night shift workers loading up pallets on their vans. I sniffed. I could smell the tinge of iron in the air. I could almost taste it on my lips. I licked my dry, cracked lips and decided the only way to do this was to make a grab and run for it. The food was becoming too irresistible. I watched them hack and sever the flesh like a starved animal, just waiting for the opportune moment to sink my teeth in to it.

'Break time!' I heard the supervisor yell from the portacabin. Great. Just in time. I just hoped I wouldn't get caught as I had no idea how to explain to them the reason why I was stealing meat.

I had my eye on the box that was slightly cast in the shadow. Hunger was now getting the best of me and I bolted for it. Even with my quick pace, I couldn't dodge the attention of the Rottweiler tied up to the streetlight by the security office.

'Shhiitt!' I paused for a brief moment, giving the dog a nasty glare with my eyes, hoping it would somehow shut him up. It didn't work and he began barking at me even more. Slowly I backed away to the stack of empty wooden pallets, when I just happened to glance up to see the door opening.

'Who's here?' The security man came yelling out of the door. I crouched down behind the pallet in front of me as he shone his torch over in my direction.

'There's nothing here you great big mutt,' he shouted to the dog. I heard the dog whine and whimper to itself as the security guard went back into the office. I peered over the box and saw his silhouette sipping on his drink through the window.

That was far too close.

After a few bites, I returned to Blaze's van. I pulled the door open and saw Blaze sitting there looking somewhat spooked out.

'Are you okay?' I asked. Hoping he hadn't seen me eating. He had both hands gripped onto the steering wheel and was looking out of the windshield. He turned on the ignition and put his foot down on the gas.

'Get the fuck in now,' he demanded. He sounded like he was in a hurry.

'Blaze, what's up?'

'You'll never fucking guess man. You'd never believe it,' he said, waving his arms about the place.

'What? What is it?'

'A vampire, a foul smelling, blood sucking bastard vampire, he had fangs and everything. I was fucking scared man, for a few seconds I thought he was you.' he shouted, pointing at me.

I slumped back against the seat feeling shocked with what I just heard.

'Me?' I said, forcing a weak smile.

It wasn't possible that he saw me just now, I didn't shift. 'Are you sure it wasn't a trick or treater?' I said, remembering he mentioned it was Halloween soon. 'Y'know, someone dressed up?'

'Well, if he was, he was one hell of a scary one; I would've given him a pint just to get rid of the stench!'

'Where did you see him?' I said feeling alarmed.

'Not long after you went to do whatever. I saw him walk past the bloody window and the fucking freak even had the balls to smirk at me.'

'Must've been someone having a laugh, I mean vampires don't exist right?' I said, wondering what his response would be.

'Of course you're right, vampires don't exist. Then it must be too many late night horror films then or I'm still fucking pissed and seeing things.'

I was still taken aback by Blaze's over-reaction to the vampire he saw at the docks. I tried to contend myself with the fact that it was almost Halloween and people were more than likely to be having parties, but was it? I didn't really want to think about it too much now. The stereo in the van was blasting out some 80's Gothic music as we cruised down the almost empty freeway.

The interior of the van was amassed with cd's and empty fast food wrappers. It was also stinking of stale cigarette smoke, which was making me retch on the quiet, so I unwound the window.

The conversation quickly turned about me. I wondered how long he would stave off his curiosity for.

'So...have you been here a while then?'

'No, I only arrived this morning.'

'Really? Oh, so you got family here, in New York?'

'No to that either.'

'Right, well I guess I'll have to show you around then. So who was that guy you were speaking to? He seemed like he was in some kind of a hurry?'

'That was Stride and I think he's always in a hurry.' How could I tell him he was a vampire hunter for real? I don't think it would've gone down very well after what he had seen. 'He was um, travelling with me.'

I didn't think I was a very good liar but he looked as if he believed me.

'Oh right. You know, I can't help thinking about that dude I saw earlier. The so-called vampire. It was really freaky man, I've never seen anything so life like. The make-up was awesome, but, what in the hell was he doing down there? It's quite a way from the city, unless...'

'Unless what?'

'Well, unless there was stuff going on down there, y'know, like you said, but there didn't appear to be any parties going on.'

'Maybe someone from the slaughterhouse saw you in the van and decided to play a practical joke on you.' I shrugged.

'How do you know about the slaughterhouse when you have never been here before?'

Shit

'Er, well it's not hard to avoid the stench, y'know.'

'Hm, yeah I suppose so.'

'So just chill out alright.'

I turned to look him and I could see his hands were shaking on the steering wheel.

'Yeah, I meant to ask you, why did you think it was me? What did he say...do?'

'He just looked like you. It was weird. Same kinda hair, facial features, apart from the fangs and the yellowish tint he had in his eyes.'

'His eyes were yellow?' Oh for fuck sake this was getting too weird. It was either a very good impersonator or my mind was playing tricks with me. Perhaps I did shift and didn't know. I don't know if that was even possible but who knows...I was in a foreign land. It was best not to say anymore to him until I spoke with Stride.

'Yeah, thinking on it, it could've been really awesome contacts. I think he would've been great in our music video though,' he roared with nervous laughter. 'Perhaps I ought to drive back and get his number.'

CHAPTER TEN

My head ached so badly. I sat myself up on the black leather sofa and
looked around at the cramped apartment. How did I get here, was all I
could think. Desperately I tried to remember the events from last night,
which led me here, but my head was still a bit foggy from all the
alcohol I was drinking. That much I did remember. But it's so quiet
here, I wondered. I was feeling quite alarmed as the place was thriving
with people from the club last night. I got up from the sofa and
frantically searched the room for traces of blood. My paranoia was
certainly now on overdrive. 'Fuck! I hope I didn't kill anyone,' I
muttered to myself as I threw the cushions off the sofa.

'Are you alright in there?'

Startled, I turned around to see Blaze looking half-asleep leaning
against the doorframe

'Blaze! You're ok?'

I have never been so relieved. Part of me was fretting that I had
drunkenly sired a few vampires last night.

'Yeah man, are you? You look like you've lost something?' he said,
taking a sip on his coffee.

I stood amongst the coffee table and the sofa that was perched besides
the window. I opened the blind, hoping I could somehow change the
subject. 'That's a big drop,' I said, looking down at the early morning
New York traffic.

'Yeah it is, don't tell me you can't remember anything from last
night?' he grinned.

I felt so ashamed I couldn't hold my drink, let alone not being able to
remember if I ate anyone or not.

'Er, I guess I drank much more than I should have.' It was a pitiful
excuse, I know.

'Well I say that's a good thing, because we're about to become
international rock stars. We'll be having a drink for breakfast, dinner
and fucking supper, I can feel it.'

'What?'

'Yeah, if this trial works out with you, we're gonna hit the big time.
Don't tell me you can't remember agreeing to try out with the band

later? Fucking hell man I thought I was a bad drunk,' he exclaimed as he walked back into the kitchen.

What have I done? I don't remember agreeing to anything, hell I don't even know if I can actually sing a note. I picked up my jacket and walked through the hall into the kitchen where Blaze was standing by the coffee machine.

'Want a coffee?' he asked quite cheerily for someone this time of morning.

'I don't drink it.'

'You're sure? I need about four cups before I can function properly.' As he was about to pour another mugful the phone rang.

'Fucking hell, it's only 8am and already the phone's hot.'
I pulled a stool out by the breakfast bar and sat down, trying my hardest not to overhear, which by my standards was impossible. I recognised the voice instantly, it was April and she sounded as if she was distressed by something. On the bar, placed in a neat pile was a stack of magazines. I pulled the top one off and flicked through it. Images of half-naked women peered up at me. Grinning to myself, I flicked a glance up at Blaze who was pacing about the kitchen in a ripped Slayer t-shirt. I could tell by his face it wasn't good news.

'Are you sure sis, do you want us to come down?'

'No, the police are asking questions and stuff, I call back later with any news.'

'Ok, as long as you're sure...'
Blaze put his mobile down on the worktop and looked at me. His face was pale.

'Jeez man, April's boss was murdered last night.'

'Really?' I sat upright feeling a little edgy. 'Do they know how? Who did it, even?' It did cross my mind for a minute if I did it.

'Nah, they reckon it was someone after some artifact that was shipped over for the exhibit.'

'Exhibit?'

'Yeah, April is the assistant curator at the museum and is also the brains of the family. Wow,' he sighed, 'I just can't believe it.'

'Yeah, neither can I,' I said rather nervously.
For Some odd reason I had a sneaky suspicion all this was all connected with the Book of The Dead. Someone was definitely on my

trail and it was only a matter of time before I was going to be found out.

'Do you know what they were after?' I asked Blaze, who was leaning over the kitchen worktop sipping on his coffee.

'Erm, some book, not sure what, but it came from Egypt.'

Oh hell, Stride was legit. Now I had no reason to dismiss anything he told me last night. My undead life was now in trouble. I had to find these people before they find me. At least I had one advantage over them, I was a Vampire, but something told me not to underestimate them. I stumbled off the stool and picked up my jacket. 'I, um, better go.' I said. I didn't have any excuse for him, nothing that would've made sense anyhow. I just couldn't risk putting Blaze's life in jeopardy too.

'Where are you going?'

'It's a long story. It's best if I leave.'

'Hey man, what's up with you?' he said, chasing after me.

I paused in the hallway clutching onto my jacket. I could feel the anger rising in me. Just nothing could go right for me if I wished.

'You really won't understand...' I said, clenching my teeth.

'I might. C'mon, you have to give the band a chance. All I need is one freakin' break in this life.'

'You and I both, but you don't know me, how can you trust me, huh? I don't even trust in myself most of the time.'

'I'm a good judge of character...besides; wouldn't you have slashed my throat last night if you were so bad?'

He did have a valid point. Besides, I was drunk anyhow. And wouldn't it be better to stick around. It seemed to me if things were happening for a reason. Not that I was a great believer in fate, but the Ankh had more power and knowledge than I ever could imagine, I had to trust in it.

'Ok,' I hesitated. 'But don't ask too many questions, I just don't have the answers to give you right now.'

Blaze shrugged.

'Sure, in your own time ok.'

CHAPTER ELEVEN

I was feeling so guilty. Blaze had kindly allowed me to stay at his apartment until I sorted something out. It has been a week already and I was feeling rather uncomfortable about staying here under false pretences. Sure, it was all quiet on the 'Stride' front and I was thankful I wasn't walking the streets with Jafar about, but somehow it didn't feel quite right as Blaze had not showed any sign in presuming I was anything different from what I said I was. It struck me as odd he didn't even show a hint of fear when he was around me.

For the past week, I have sat idly in the apartment while Blaze went out to work as a car mechanic. I didn't want to face things right now. I even had to drag myself to slaughterhouse for food every night. The excuses I had to make were becoming ridiculous. I couldn't exactly say to Blaze I'm going out for a drink, he would've only have dragged me to the nearest bar and unless they had blood on tap, it wasn't going to do anything for my cravings.

Today, as usual I slumped back on Blaze's sofa, armed with the TV remote, flicking over the music channels until I could find some decent song to listen too. Music was becoming an escape for me these days, especially with the band and the music lessons with Blaze that would go on until early hours in the morning.

After a few hours of peace, the reality of what was happening around me soon plagued my thoughts again. I took a sip on my cup of blood and rested my head against the cushion. The curtains were drawn and a soft rock song was playing quietly in the background. I started to reminisce about my mother. She was a human that had been changed by my father. It was probably why I have always been so curious about humans and their nature, and that maybe, despite my urge to suck their blood, I perhaps held some of their traits deep inside me. Staying with Blaze only affirmed my desire to return the Ankh before anyone would steal it. Yet, my meeting with Stride made me re-evaluate the fact it wasn't going to be an easy task There was something else I had to do, for that I was certain.

Almost as I entered into a state of calmness, I heard keys rattling in the lock.

Blaze walked through the door followed by April. Whether it was the human side to me showing, I don't know, but I shot up from the sofa wracked with nerves.

'Are you alright man?' Blaze asked as he rushed to the kitchen with a box of food.

That left me with April, standing in an awkward stance gazing at the poor woman who didn't know where to look. She smiled at me and put her bag of books down on the chair. A few seconds lingered and then she suddenly spoke.

'Hi, so we meet again. Um, so how has it been, staying with my brother? Is he still a filthy bastard that leaves his clothes all over the floor?' she laughed.

Realising that I was now staring at her and making her feel uncomfortable; I averted my gaze from her beautiful dark hair that was tied into a ponytail, and looked down towards my feet. I've never felt so nervous around a woman before and I think my inexperience was beginning to show.

'Of course he's still a dirty bastard, but then I tell him, I'm not your mother, so don't expect me to clean up you're crap,' I laughed, 'that usually works.'

April laughed.

'Oh jeez, you're so funny. It's no wonder you two get on, you're so alike,' she said and walked through the kitchen.

Alike, I thought. Nothing could've been further from the truth.

I followed her out into the kitchen where Blaze was serving out the food. I wanted to ask April about the exhibit but now didn't seem like the right time.

'Do you want any food?' Blaze asked chewing on a mouthful of chicken.

'Er, I'm not fussed,' I lied. I didn't really want to.

'Do you know what? I've just realised something I've hardly seen you eat a thing this week…in fact I go as far as saying you haven't ate anything at all.'

I watched him plate up the food as I tried to think of an excuse I could palm him off on. I was certain he had an inkling that I was different.

'Are you a veggie Jyrki?' April asked, looking up at me with a smile.

'Um, no,' I smirked, 'just not used to foreign food.'

'Foreign!' Blaze spluttered, 'don't you have chicken and noodles in Finland for fuck sake? Come on, try a bit, I'm not gonna fucking charge ya.'

'Ok, ok give it here then,' I said leaning against the kitchen worktop. The plate of noodles and chicken, which was promptly shoved in my face, didn't look too appetising, I must admit, but reluctantly, to 'appear human,' tonight I took the plate and forced a mouthful down. It wasn't that I couldn't eat the food. I just wasn't use to the texture. I took another mouthful as they both watched me curiously.

'Yay, see that wasn't so difficult now, was it?' April clapped.

'Now I class you as an honorary American bro. Here's a beer, get that down ya neck too.'

'Give him a chance to chew the food first Blaze,' April laughed I spluttered, almost choking on a chicken bone.

'Oh jeez man, you are one of a kind.'

'I probably am.' I said feeling quite embarrassed to be eating in front of April.

'Hey April, have you heard this guy sing yet?'

'No obviously not. I haven't been here for a week have I? I've been busy revising for exams and sorting out stuff from work. We're still no closer to finding out who killed Dr. Matthews though.'

'Really? I thought they had a lead?'

'No. Nothing solid yet. Anyway enough about work ok.'

'You should take a week off sis.'

'No, I need to revise for my doctorate.'

'You need a life outside work as well, y'know. That's all I'm saying.'

'Jyrki, I swear sometimes he thinks he's my father,' April said, taking another mouthful of food.

'I think he's right, you do need to take a break. Are you coming to our show next week?'

'Yeah, I wouldn't miss that for anything.'

'Oh I forgot to say, Jonesy asked us to meet him down the pub later. April, are you coming?'

'Yeah I suppose so, just to shut you up.'

'Jyrki?'

I couldn't very well say no, especially since April would be there.

'Sure, but I need a change of clothes first.'

'Well, I'll have to meet you both there. I must take those library books back first before I get another $20 fine,' April said.

CHAPTER TWELVE

Things were happening in my life pretty quickly since arriving in New York. Almost like a succession of events that were playing out towards a grand finale. Not wanting to dwell on such things right now, I sat on the bed and pressed the CD player to come on. The rock music was drowning out my thoughts, which were becoming very erratic lately. I was drinking twice the amount of blood than I was used to, just so that I didn't accidently attack Blaze in the nights. I had wondered what Blaze must've thought about me though, as I didn't actually need any sleep. A few times now, he had caught me sitting on the sofa in a hypnotic trance-like state. It's something us vampires do for time-out. Sometimes I wished I could have had more time out from all that was going on with Stride and the prophecy. Lately, it was all I thought about.

Blaze popped his head around the door.

'Here's a t shirt you can have,' he said throwing it on the bed. 'It's one of ours, we wear them to promote the band. Do you think you're up to singing tonight? Thought we could do a small show there just for practice? I'll introduce you to the guys then?'

'Err, yeah sure,' I grinned. I was looking forward to tonight as I knew April would be there. I took another glimpse at myself in the mirror and ruffled up my dark damp hair. I did look slightly paler than the average human, but that along with my dark hair and blue eyes, is probably what attracted the females to me anyway. Their attraction to me is more than likely what makes the temptation to drink their blood even more difficult to resist, especially when they were under the influence of alcohol, and couldn't decide on whether I was a friend or foe. Tonight, I had to be on my best behaviour so there would be no chance of a repeat of what happened in Helsinki.

I took the black t-shirt from the bed and pulled it over my pale, slightly masculine chest. There was a sense of acceptance and belonging attached to it, which made me feel a little more human tonight.

'Are you ready?' Blaze hollered from the door.

'Yeah sure, let me just get my jacket.'

'We'll walk, yeah?'

'Sure.'

I felt like a brisk walk anyway. My nerves needed calming down before I was about to sing in front of a real crowd for the first time. As we stepped out of the door, the noise from the police sirens that went passed and the drunken antics of the people that were around were making it impossible for me to soothe my nerves anyway, in fact it was just adding to my tension.

'It's just another normal Saturday evening, don't worry.'

'No, I'm not worried about that,' I said, pointing to a man being arrested.

'Hey, the show is gonna be great ok, just chill out. I don't know what the fuck you're worried about though you have it all, the chicks are going love you!' he laughed obviously clocking on to my nervousness. We must've walked about a half of mile up the road when Blaze pointed out the club.

'Here we go, Crowley's, the best live music venue this side of town. I'll introduce you to everyone, c'mon.'

I walked through the doors, brushing my way past a couple of youngsters sipping on their beers. They looked up at me with a glint of admiration. Was it because I was in the band I pondered or did they know what I really was.

My tall frame and dark brooding good looks surpassed many of the people here, almost as if it was invite to everyone to look up at me as I made my way to the bar.

'Jyrki?' I felt a tug on my arm.

'This is Jonesy, our drummer. He's from London and has played with some of the best metal bands out there. We're lucky to have him.'

'Hiya mate. It's nice to finally meet ya. Blaze mentioned he had found us a singer like, so you've been practicing with Blaze? How's it going?'

I was relieved he took to me; I guess some people could see past the horror of what I really am, which was intriguing. 'Nice to meet you too,' I said holding my hand out in gesture. I looked at him studiously. The tattoos and piercings were quite an elaborate piece of body art I had ever seen. There couldn't have been an inch of him besides his face that wasn't inked.

'It's mostly friends here tonight, so I wouldn't worry about fucking up,' he smirked.

'Friends?' I said, glancing around at the hundred or so people.

'Yep, the band has a small following here. Before the last singer quit, we were doing quite well, we were so close to signing with a label.'

'Then I guess I have a lot to live up too.'

'You sure do, but no pressure,' he laughed.

Then I saw April standing by the bar talking to some female friends. My attention quickly diverted to her.

'Err, sorry I'm just gonna get a drink, I'll see you later yeah?'

'Yeah sure man, we're on at ten!'

There must've been some sort of connection between us. Before I could say anything, she turned towards me and smiled quite coyly. Although my intentions were more than honorable, I couldn't help but feel there was an underlay of a much darker fate that brought us together. I must ask her about the exhibition tonight, I thought as I gazed at her sweet smile. I had a sneaky feeling she was going to be of some help.

'Do you want to sit down?' she hollered in my ear.

My hearing was good enough without anyone resorting to shouting, but she wasn't to know that. She pointed towards an empty table at the corner of the room.

'Yeah, sure, just let me get a drink do you want one?'

'Oh ok, I'll have a vodka and coke then,' she smiled.

I pushed my way through the crowd to get to the bar, feeling much more relaxed than I had done in a while, for once the vampire wasn't central in my mind and I was actually having one of the best nights of my life.

'Excuse me?' I shouted over to the barman. He was busy pulling a pint for someone else but the sound of urgency in my voice caught his attention.

'What do you want?'

'A beer and a vodka and coke.'

'Can't you see I'm serving someone? Hold on.'

Over the noise of inane chatter and the music, I heard Blaze drunkenly shout...

'Aw come on now, he's our new singer, serve him next Craig or I'm gonna charge you double for the gig!'

There was a roar of laughter from the punters stood around the bar.

'Yeah, and when you sign that record deal you've been going on about for the last two years we're gonna have to discuss how you would like to pay your tab. With interest!'

The laughter spread from the bar to the rest of the club. I soaked up the feel good atmosphere and smiled along with the rest of the humans.

'Here you go,' I said to April. I placed the glass down on the table and sat down on the chair opposite. An awkward silence lingered. I noticed she looked at me a few times before quickly glancing away. She wasn't like the other females I had encountered. Her response to me as a vampire was fairly relaxed, which I found enchanting. I decided to engage in some small talk to help her overcome her shyness.

'Do you usually come to see Blaze playing?'

She put her glass down and looked at me, relieved I had made the first move.

'All the time. He was so upset after the last singer had quit. They were about to be offered a contract by a small independent label, but it fell through when he couldn't find a replacement on time. Since you came along, he's been a lot happier, as if his life is finally getting back on track.'

'Well, it's the least I can do since he offered me a place to stay. Y'know, I wasn't sure about this singing business at first but to tell you the truth, I really am enjoying it. We never had music back home, not like what you have. Well if you can count the birds' s--'

'Really? No music whatsoever?'

Perhaps I shouldn't had said that, even though it was the truth.

'I'm kidding with you,' I laughed.

She blushed.

'Oh I knew you were,' she said.

I took another sip of my drink and then undid my jacket.

'What's that?' April gasped, pointing at my chest.

'What's what?'

I looked down and there was my Ankh was resting on my new fresh t-shirt. Shit. I had meant to tuck it under before I came out.

'I know it's an Ankh, but that one I recognise.'

Alarm bells rang in my head. I quickly tucked it under hoping she would change the subject. Her face became inquisitive, as if she was studying me. She then met my gaze and her eyes widened. Her mouth was slightly open ajar and just as she was about to say something else Blaze slammed his empty glass down on our table.

'Hey, we're on soon, come over here will you I want to introduce you to more people. Mind if I take him sis?'

April didn't say anything, she just kept staring at me which I found very unnerving.

I didn't have much of a choice in the matter. He grabbed my arm and literally pulled me off the chair. I had just a moment to take my drink and whisper, 'Sorry.' to April, for whatever good that would do.

She definitely knew something. There was no denying it, not with her background in Ancient Egypt. Still, she may have recognised the Ankh, but that doesn't mean she knew of its significance or even about the vampires. No, there was no possible way she could know.

'Are you ready for this, man?' Blaze asked as we walked back to the bar.

The crowd had now gathered by the front of the stage, cheering us on. Jonesy and the guys were already tuning up the guitars. Blaze gulped down the remainder of his drink and patted me on the back.

'Thanks man, I know I'm drunk, I know I shouldn't even open my fucking mouth when I'm drunk, but YOU are fucking awesome, so come on let's hit the stage and create some Rock n' Roll mayhem!' he slurred.

I had to laugh. He was absolutely wrecked. I suspected the excitement had really got to him of being able to play again.

The lights dimmed, and the hundred or so people that had come here to see us began clapping in succession to the drumbeat. I stood behind the microphone and felt an electrifying tingle throughout my body. I grasped the microphone stand and began to nod my head to the beat. I pushed my sunglasses up allowing my long dark hair to fall across my face. Blaze strummed the first chord of our new song and the crowd cheered for more. Izzy soon came in with the bass and the crowd went wilder, the stage lights illuminated blue behind me and as I came in with the first line of the song, I felt a sense of pride and enjoyment as I've never experienced before, but how long would it last was anyone's guess.

The first song ended and the crowd chanted for more. No one was more surprised than I was. I brushed back my sweat soaked hair feeling relieved I didn't fuck up once.

'Hey!' Blaze shouted through the microphone. There was a bit of feedback that made me wince. 'I just want to take a moment to introduce you to The Black Stone's newest member...Jyrki!'

The crowd clapped and roared, and the feeling of acceptance amongst these humans only instilled my faith in myself against the Egyptians.

I looked out on to the crowd and saw April talking on her mobile. We were almost finishing our set and despite enjoying myself, I was eager to talk with her.

CHAPTER THIRTEEN

'You my friend were fucking awesome last night, did you hear the crowd?' Blaze asked sipping on his first coffee of the morning.

I had no idea what was in that coffee of his but he looked as hyper as I was when I tried human blood for the first time. I had no desire to go there again, that's for sure.

'Yeah, I was there, you know. I still have this awful ringing noise in my ears to prove it,' I said, as I sat down on the sofa. We hadn't long arrived back at the flat and I was feeling quite hungry.

'Do you know what happened to April last night? She left pretty early didn't she?' he said.

'I saw her talking on the phone before our set ended. She looked like she was spooked out by something,' I mumbled to him as I rested my head in my hands. Last night was the only real break I've had from everything, I even felt normal for once. Now, today everything came crashing back into my consciousness, or was this what they called a hangover.

'Are you alright man?' Blaze laughed as he began picking up the remainder of the glass bottles on the floor.

'Do you think you could go easy on the clattering? My head is pounding.'

'No problem. So what did you say about April? She left after she got a call? Do you know that fucking job of hers they have her running around at all hours of the bloody day and night lately.'

'They sure do.'

'Well I know it's early, but as it's my day off I was thinking of hitting the studio later to work on some new songs. The guys are gonna be there too. Are you coming or do you have other stuff to be getting on with?'

'I'll er, come with you,' I said as I sat back against the sofa. The curtains were still drawn and the music was playing low in the background. I wondered how long this peace would last for.
As usual, I asked Blaze to drop me off at the docks. I made up an excuse of having to pay someone back down there for a loan I had. It was the only way he wouldn't ask so many questions. Questions I just

didn't have the answers for right now.

'Let me check something, hang on,' I said to Blaze who was waiting impatiently by the door of the foyer. 'My sunglasses. Where are they?' I said, checking my pockets.

'They are inside your jacket pocket. I saw you put them in there on the way out,' he tutted. 'What do you want them for eh? The sun ain't that strong today mind you. Are you sure you're not a vampire, I mean, you bloody act like one?'

'And what if I was?' I said half-jokingly.

'Do you know what? That wouldn't surprise me at all. Hey, I thought we'd take my car today, you like?' he said pointing at a black 1970's Mustang.

'Yeah, that's a fine car,' I said, trying to show some interest.

'My pride and joy mate, but it won't be for much longer if I don't make some serious cash.'

'Yeah,' I looked up at him. 'How's that?'

'Ah. well, the firm I'm working for is losing money, before long they'll be going into liquidation and I'll be out on the dole again. Unless this band gets anywhere soon I'll have to kiss goodbye to this beauty. Okay that's enough about my shitty life c'mon, let's go'

It was a short drive to Manhattan, but due to the volume of traffic this morning things were taking a lot longer than expected. I kept fidgeting with the radio dial, just to keep my mind off the blood.

'Are you always this annoying? Is this why you don't have a girlfriend?' Blaze said, sounding pissed off with me.

'Sorry, I didn't realise I was being a nuisance. Anyway I haven't exactly seen you with a woman since I've met you either?' I smirked. Blaze scoffed and looked around the car in embarrassment.

'Well, I did have, up until three months ago. The bitch left me for my old singer,' he said, 'I caught her in bed with him after one of our shows. I couldn't play for a while after that, I was a fucking wreck, but I'm over it now…life goes on.'

I didn't want to show him I was laughing, so I covered my mouth and looked out of the window. 'Sorry to hear that, really. I guess I have a lot to learn about women too.'

Blaze laughed. 'No point in trying to work them out mate, when you think you have them sussed out you're back to square one again. So, there's no women in your life then?'

There has only ever been one female vampire, my mother. For some reason the demon doesn't hold very well in the female form. 'No,' I replied, 'it's just me.'

'So, there have been no girlfriends then. How do you cope with no sex?'

'I don't, that's the point. I endure it.'

'Oh right. I bet it can't be easy though. I always thought vampires like you were sex mad?' he said jokingly.

Of course we are, I thought. We require the same basic human pleasures, but what with the agreement and not being able to leave the island, our indulgences did not come into it. The protection of the Ankh was far greater than our needs and wants. I had to lie to him and tell him I lived a very sheltered life.

'So now you're gonna make up for it then?' Blaze laughed. 'I can introduce you to some ladies if you want?'

'Thanks, but there may already be someone.'

'Oh yeah, you kept that quiet. Anyone I know?'

'Er, I don't think so,' I lied.

After my usual drink at the slaughterhouse, we eventually pulled up into what looked like a ghost town. The buildings were rundown and mostly empty. Apart from a few hobo's standing around a trashcan drinking alcohol, there was no other visible signs of life.

'Here we go, I know it ain't exactly paradise city but it'll do us until the big bucks come rolling in, if they ever do,' Blaze said almost apologetically.

I got out of the car and pulled my sunglasses off to cast an eye over the building. To look at their rehearsal studio you wouldn't think it was fit enough for rats let alone humans. I don't know where I fitted in categorically wise, but I guess I was nothing more than vermin myself.

I laughed. I hadn't noticed the worn out sign just above the door. 'This was a sex shop?'

Blaze obviously caught onto my amusement and smirked.

'Yep, that's why we chose it. C'mon, I'll introduce you to the guys again, only this time, with no alcohol involved. Well, maybe not for you.'

Blaze pushed the wooden door to open but it kept being wedged.

'Damn this fucking thing. I've lost count how many times this has happened.'

'Want me to try?'

'Nah. It's ok. Could you go back to the car and get my guitar from the trunk?'

'Yeah sure, got the key?'

I walked back to the car when I noticed a silver BMW drive slowly up the road towards us. For the first time in a while, I felt very uneasy. I squinted my eyes to see who was driving but the blacked out windows wasn't giving too much away. I just only hope Stride would find me soon, as there was so much more he needed to explain.

'Finally!' I heard Blaze yell.

I looked back towards the building; Blaze had managed to get the door open and was lying flat on his back on the floor.

'What happened to you?' I laughed

'I've got to get a new door as soon as possible. That,' he pointed to the door, 'is fucking lethal.'

I helped him to his feet and passed him his guitar. I tried to make out everything was fine, but there was the worry of the mysterious car and more importantly who was in it that was really bothering me. The others, who I had only really known from Father as looking nothing like us, was the only means I had to go on. I doubted they would be out in daylight, so I had to contend with the fact they must've been what Stride was talking about.

I was lost in thought.

'Hey!'

'Oh sorry, I was miles away.'

Blaze shot me that look he did when I first met him, the curious 'I know you are different look, but I can't say.' kind of thing. It would be great to share this burden with someone but I really didn't want to put all this on him now, not with the problems he had.

We walked through the narrow corridor and up the creaky staircase which looked like it was about to collapse under our weight. It did cross my mind if this building was at all safe. It certainly looked like it was ready for demolishing.

The band had already started tuning up as we walked through the door. All eyes were on me.

I did feel a bit uncomfortable; especially since I didn't know what in the hell I got up to last night.

'Alright?'

I looked at them and they looked at me. A few awkward seconds of silence past and then they all burst out laughing.

'Man, you were hilarious last night.'

'Er...' I looked towards Blaze who obviously taken their side and was laughing along too. 'What did I do?'

'Oh it wasn't what you did but what you said. You are a fantastic storyteller mate, especially on the Bud.'

'Really?' I frowned. 'What did I say?'

'Well, what didn't you say? He laughed. 'Apparently you are a vampire that had to leave Finland because you were being hunted by some guys that are after the Ankh of yours. And if that didn't sound so fucked up it also allows you to walk in daylight!'
He laughed so hard, I didn't feel that they took me seriously anyhow, so I wasn't really concerned.

'Ah, I see,' I smiled, feeling slightly embarrassed by my overactive mouth. 'I guess I should stick to soft drinks from now on then.'

CHAPTER FOURTEEN

It had been a long day and my voice was becoming a little achy with all
the re-takes we had to keep doing. I was pretty much looking forward
to getting back home and chilling out for the rest of the evening. As I
sat on the swivel chair listening to the track we had just recorded, I saw
Blaze flinch at the corner of my eye.

'Did you hear that? Blaze nudged me. 'It sounded like a howling of a
wolf?' he said, jumping off his chair.

'What?' I took the headphones off and walked towards the window.

'There's a wolf in New York? Jonesy laughed. 'Blaze how much
booze did you put in your coffee?'

'You said you heard a wolf. Are you sure it wasn't a dog?' I said.

'Nah. It was most definitely a wolf. Man, that was fucking creepy,' he
said peering out of the window.

I looked down onto the dark, desolate street. The rain pelted down as
usual into the puddles that glowed orange under the street lamps. A
frown drew across my face, as I was almost sure I saw a shadow
disappear into the alleyway between the two buildings opposite. Blaze
could've been right, but the guy hasn't slept in almost 48 hours. I knew
humans needed sleep, just like I needed time out, but I just felt a
strange sensation come over me, as if I was being watched again.
I backed away from the window and picked up my jacket.

'You're leaving? Don't tell me you're spooked out by imaginary
wolves too?' Jonesy laughed, almost dropping his guitar he was tuning
up.

'Fucking hell,' I heard him yell, catching the neck of his Gibson
before it hit the floor.

'That's what happens when you mock people,' I said, smiling at his
demise.

'Wait for me!'
Blaze looked startled. He picked up his keys and ran towards me at the
door.

'Where are you going?' Do you need a lift? Because I don't fancy
driving through here tonight. We can finish up the tracks another time.'

'Ok, just er, drop me off...'

'Down the docks?' He said, finishing my sentence.

'You know me too well, but er, no, not tonight. I need to find Stride. You know, that guy who was with me at the bar that night? I haven't seen him since and he owes me something.'

If anything, he owed me an explanation.

'Oh yeah, I remember. Do you know where he lives?'

'No, I've no idea, but I've got a feeling he'll be looking for me tonight though.'

Blaze instantly noticed my dark mood in the car and began asking questions again.

'Is everything really alright with you? I know you said you didn't want to talk about stuff, but I hope you won't mind me saying this but there's something about you I can't put my finger on.'

'I'm not an American?' I laughed.

'Funny! No I meant, you are different, you just seem different, oh never mind,' he shrugged and regained his focus on the road.

I looked at him and was about to tell him the truth but I just couldn't get the words out. I mean, how do you explain to someone that every belief he held about the world was wrong? Oh Blaze by the way I'm a vampire and I'm sitting next to you in the car. I don't think that would go down very well. Humans, I come to believe, lived in their own little world, a world that shielded itself away from the impossible and unimaginable. Why should I be the one to destroy his ignorance?

'Who the fuck is that following us?'

'Huh?'

'That bike behind us, it's almost blinding me with its headlight.' Blaze snapped

I looked into the wing mirror and could see a hand movement gesturing us to pullover.

'Pullover, its Stride.'

'Him? How the fuck does he know where to find us?'

Blaze swerved the car off the road and pulled up onto the pavement almost knocking down a couple of prostitutes leaning against the streetlight. I got out of the car quickly when one of the women began walking towards me.

'Looking for business boys?' she said touching my arm.

'Not tonight love,' Stride said, pushing her away from me.

I looked at her in her tight blue dress and overdone face and scowled. I was hungry and there was nothing I would've liked more than a cup of fresh blood right now.

'Ok, ok chill, you freak. I wouldn't have done you anyway,' she said as she walked off.

Stride shook his head and watched her as she walked back to her friend.

'What a filthy slag eh?' he said, shaking his head.

'Stride!' I said relieved. I was thirsty and I was hoping he would have something to drink on him. 'Where the hell have you been? You can't just walk off like that and not tell me where I can find you?'

'Why? What's the problem?'

'What's the problem? Something has been watching me tonight?'

'Watching you? Um, Look, I do apologise okay. It was wrong of me to leave you there, but my life is in danger too, just for helping you. So, tell Slash in there to follow me back to my place alright. Jyrki, can you trust him?

I turned around to look at Blaze sat in the driver seat fiddling about with his mobile.

'Yeah, I can't see him being a problem.'

'Right then, follow me and see you in a bit.'

'Sure, oh do you have anything for me to drink?'

'Of course, I'm stocked up on the stuff.'

I turned around and got back into the car.

'We need to follow Stride, step on it.'

'Ok, I just tried April's phone again and there's still no answer. This is really weird.'

CHAPTER FIFTEEN

'Welcome to my personal hell!' Stride said, gesturing us towards his warehouse.

'Is this where you live?' I asked. I was trying my hardest not to laugh at the unsightly, rusted warehouse that seemed so out of place amongst all the thriving businesses down the docks.

'Yeah, turns out this little old tin can was a lot cheaper than renting out a flat in the city, you like? I bumped into some old geezer in an English bar in Brooklyn and he mentioned he had a place for rent, so he's letting me have this for two hundred dollars a month. A pretty good bargain eh?'

'Hm, not bad,' Blaze nodded, obviously wondering what we were doing here.

I could see Blaze seemed a little worried by the intense frown he had across his face as he looked around the area. The only road in and out of this place was deserted, and lit by a few sparse streetlights. He began to fidget with his keys in his pocket and was looking rather nervous.

'Look, do you want to leave?'

The last thing I wanted was for him to find out the truth about me.

'No, he can't,' Stride ordered.

'Why not?' I fumed.

'I specifically asked you if you could trust him and you said you could. Now, I don't think it's wise if he left right now because if we were being followed, it is more than likely they'll go after him. You don't want that on your conscience do you?'

'What do you mean by being followed?'

'Fucking hell Jyrki, by the S.O. Y'know,' he winked.

He did have a point. I could not risk putting Blaze in any danger.

'Hey guys, I'm getting freaked out here, would someone please tell me what is going on?'

Stride and I exchanged glances.

'You tell him...'

'No, you tell him, he's your mate. I don't want the responsibility of breaking up a friendship.'

'Oh for fuck sake, are you drug dealers or something?' Blaze asked.

'Er, not quite,' I said trying not to laugh.

Stride sniggered to himself as he pushed the rusty door open. 'Boy, are you gonna be in a for a fucking surprise.'

He was right. The fluorescent lights flickered a few times before coming on fully and when they did, Blaze and I stood at the doorway with open mouths.

'What ya think?' Stride asked so proudly.

'Erm, what is this place man? It looks like you've ransacked a library!' Blaze said, looking quite stunned.

'Ransacked?' I looked at Blaze, and then back at the small living area that was littered with books and documents stacked on anything that could take its weight. 'Looks like you've been burgled.'

'Forgive me. I haven't cleaned up here for a while.'

Blaze laughed nervously and walked through almost tripping up on a suitcase on the floor.

'You mean, not at all.'

'Well this place is only temporary. I'm only in the States for a short while.'

It didn't take long for Blaze to notice the contents of the mad clutter either.

'Vampire books? What's this? The X files office?' he sniggered as he flicked through the dusty book.

Well at least he laughed I thought. It could've been worse.

'Stride this is crazy,' I said as I watched him pour himself a scotch. 'What exactly do you do here?'

'Sit yourselves down lads; we've got some talking to do. Hey Jyrki, he, er,' pointing to Blaze, 'knows what you are right?'

I just shook my head at him.

'Oh right, I think he's gonna need a scotch then...' and he began pouring another two glasses.

I was feeling slightly dizzy with hunger, but I tried to ignore it, as I didn't feel it was appropriate to ask for some blood in front of a human, especially one who didn't know about our existence. I was prepared to hear what Stride had to say. Did I trust him though, well, he was gaining my confidence slowly.

'Stride, what are we going to tell him. He will find out eventually?'

'Tell me what? Y'know, you guys are scaring me...'

'Hey lad, it's nothing to be concerned about, well actually it depends on the way you look at it...' Stride said, looking at me with growing concern.

Now I was feeling very weak, and must've been looking very pale in complexion, more than I did normally because Stride knew straight away what was wrong and ran to the fridge.

'You're looking like a fucking ghost Jyrki, when was your last meal?'

'What's up with him?' Blaze said, quite freaked out by the way I looked.

I sat leaning over the chair, struggling to stop the transformation, but the shakes and the smell of blood just feet away was too much to handle.

'It must've been bad blood…Stride, I can't control it…'

I glanced over towards Blaze who was staring at me from the sofa, I noticed he shifted his gaze towards the door, obviously wondering whether he should make a run for it or not.

The evil chatter in my head was slowly drowning out their voices and the darkness began to consume my entire body. The last blood I had could not have been good enough to keep me from shifting this quick. How stupid of me to think the meat alternative was going to last. I stumbled off the sofa, gripping onto the legs of the coffee table.

'Striddeee! Quick!' I growled, trying to cover my face with my jacket. But it was too late. Blaze knew something was up. He must've noticed my eyes shift to yellow. The next thing I knew I heard Blaze screaming.

'Fucckkk! Fuckkkk!'

He leapt from the sofa and backed away to the door.

'Stride, what the fucking hell is happening to him?' he yelled

'Get bloody chains by the door!' Stride screamed to Blaze 'Now!'

'What is it? What is it?'

The fangs began to come and the useless chatter that was in my head felt somewhat calmer. The demon had taken me over completely. I leapt from the floor and was just about to attack Stride trying to open a sachet of blood when I felt a stinging sensation of a glass bottle over the back of my head.

'My fucking Scotch! What did you do that for?' I heard Stride holler.

'Are you fucking serious?' I could hear Blaze scream. 'Can't you see he's a fucking monster, you stupid old bastard.'

I stumbled head first into the file cabinet, hitting all the papers he had stacked flying everywhere. Stride grabbed both my arms around my back and tried to secure them with a chain but I was far too strong for him and yanked the chain from his hands.

'Get away from me!' I scowled as I pushed Stride halfway across the room.

I swerved my body around and turned my attention to Blaze.

'Jyrki! Stay away from him! Please!' Stride begged me.

I was in my head but it wasn't me, it was almost as if I was watching myself in a mirror. I really didn't like this feeling. I had this overwhelming urge to kill and hunt. I could feel the new blood running through my veins. It was like an electrical charge pumping to every fibre of my being. I had to slow it all down, and fight off the adrenaline that was keeping the demon alive, but the voice kept telling me to kill him.

I licked my lips, laughing manically to myself as I walked slowly up to Blaze who was now struggling to open the door.

'Don't hurt me man, please, it's me Blaze, oh please don't kill me.' Every step I took, Blaze went a shade whiter. Inside, I was desperately fighting the demon off, but I had let it go on so long it was becoming an impossible task.

I slammed my hands against the metal door, trapping him between my body and the wall. I became aware of my sinister laugh echoing throughout the building. Blaze cowered down and whimpered. He looked at me with eyes begging me to let him go. I lifted him up and slammed him against the door but as the force of my arm came down, I scratched him across his cheek with my ring.

I sniffed.

'Blood!'

'Fucking hell Blaze, don't let him anywhere near the blood for Christ sake!' Stride yelled.

Almost as I went to grab Blaze, I felt a sharp tug of a chain wrap around my body. Stride pulled me with all his strength and dragged me along the floor.

'Here, take this Jyrki,' Stride said, as he emptied the sachet of blood over my mouth

I was shaking. I sucked the blood from the sachet so fast I didn't even bother to question if it was human or not.

'You've got to calm yourself down now, Jyrki, ok, come back, you got it?'

I was lying flat out on the floor feeling completely satisfied with myself.

'He, he has fangs!' Blaze whimpered from the corner.

'Of course he has bloody fangs, he's a vampire, what do you expect?' I had to laugh at Stride.

'It's not the Jyrki you know mate, don't worry, he'll be alright in a bit.' I hoped I would be okay as I was aware the vampire was still lingering on. It never use take this long for me to change back.

'What do you mean he's a vampire?' I heard Blaze whimper.

'You've seen the films right? Well you ought to know what a vampire is when you see one. But this one doesn't sparkle in the sunlight,' Stride laughed. 'You see this Ankh here? Huh? It's what keeps him safe from the sun.'

'There's no such thing as vampires.'

'Then what do you think this is?' He pointed towards me sitting like a wild animal on the floor. 'A bloody good actor? I think not.'

CHAPTER SIXTEEN

I came around slowly, not remembering much of what had happened or why I was laying down on the floor at Stride's place. I lifted my head up off the floor and was about to get up when I noticed some scratches on my arm and an empty sachet of blood beside me. 'Oh fuck, what did I do?' I said, feeling drowsy. I shot a glance towards Blaze. He was sat on the sofa shaking and looking at me as if he didn't know me. His eyes were on me and it quickly dawned on me I had almost killed him. Oh no, he knows.

Stride grabbed my arm and helped me up onto a chair.

'Are you ok? You're Jyrki now right?'

I nodded.

'Yeah, I think so. How bad was I?'

'Let's say I wouldn't want a repeat of it,' Stride said exhaustedly as he undone the chains on my hands.

I was overcome with guilt and remorse. I sat limp on the chair, full of shame for what I had done to them. I hoped there would be a better way of telling Blaze, but selfishly I felt relieved it was all over.

'Here, let's clean the blood up we can't let you walk around like that.' Whilst Stride tended to my wound, there was an awkward silence that quickly followed by a lot of pent up anger and rage from Blaze.

'It's not possible; it's just not fucking possible,' he stammered.

I lowered my head in shame, unable to look him in the eye.

I don't think 'sorry' would've sufficed. I felt like I had destroyed his childlike look upon the world.

'I, er, think we all need to talk,' Stride broke in. 'Jyrki, listen, you can't help what you are but you can help who you are, don't go beating yourself up ok, just consider it lucky I was around to help.'

'Blaze,' I paused. 'I am truly sorry you had to see that, I was going to tell you...'

'When? When you were going to eat me? Fuck sake man, I took you in, you rode in my car, you could've killed me at any time...but vampires don't exist. You are not real, how could you be real? Explain it to me, c'mon?'

I looked at Stride who was sitting on the arm of the sofa sipping on a

Scotch; he gave me an encouraging nod. I then looked towards Blaze who looked half the man he did earlier. His eyes were blood shot and his hair just hanged over his face sticking to the blood from the gash on his cheek. I hoped I would find the right words, but to put it mildly I had just destroyed the only real friendship I had. Nothing was going to make him forgive me. I decided I had to tell him the truth.

'You deserve the truth, but please don't hate me for what I am ok?'

'Hate you? You almost fucking killed me man. You know, I always suspected there was something different about you, but it never crossed my mind that you were a sideshow freak!'

Stride got up from the chair and went over to calm Blaze down.

'Blaze, you should have a drink and try and calm down alright. If only you'll listen to him...'

'Listen to him? Why in the hell couldn't you tell me this before, at least I would've had the sense to stay the hell away from him?'

There was no letup of us anger and I had to respect that.

'So, come on then, tell me, how the fuck could you be a vampire, when they only exist in the movies and fucking books...how come nobody knows about this?'

'If you calm down, he'll explain...'

Stride huffed and shook his head at me.

'Jyrki, where the fuck did you find him?'

'You, you Scottish prick was in on this too, you're just as bad as he is,' Blaze yelled, pointing a finger at me.

'I don't have the authority to say anything. Now will you calm your fucking self-down and listen to the lad,' Stride said, getting rather impatient with him.

'Lad? Don't you mean a fucking monster?'

I wasn't expecting his reaction to be this bad. I only went to get up from the chair when he flinched.

'I'm not going to hurt you alright. So do you want to know the truth or not?'

He couldn't look at me.

'Yeah, I may as well,' he said.

'Vampires,' I began, 'were created in Ancient Egypt during the reign of Ramesses, after an ancient spell that went wrong. You see, Ramesses needed an army that was powerful enough to overthrow his enemies.

So, he called upon Sekhmet, a powerful warrior goddess for help, but he received the kind of help he wasn't expecting. Sekhmet drank blood and infused her ways on to the human form. My father Amroath, was summoned to keep the Ankh, a powerful symbol of the ancient gods, safe from these creatures who were slowly taking over the whole village...'

'Ankh? What is this fucking thing good for?'

'It was soon discovered that the Ankh which hung in the tombs of Anubis, the protector of the dead, would enable us to walk in daylight. This obviously caused great concern as they started killing the whole village of Deir el-Medina. Most of the vampires were slayed by the Serpents Sword by my father, who was despite his lowly caretaker job at the temple, had once been a great warrior himself. Unfortunately, he got bitten, but his strength and resilience to the demon was recognised by the Ancient Gods, and there was born the prophecy...'
Blaze didn't look too convinced.

'What you are spouting off is all myth...'

'Yes, but even myths have their roots in facts. Why do you think the modern world knows about the vampire figure? Because of what I have just told you that's why. Your Hollywood version of the creature is myth. I am not. I am as real as you are to me right now.'

'This is bullcrap! Why doesn't anybody know anything about this huh? And why now? Why me?'

'Listen lad, I can back up everything he has told you as the truth....'
Stride piped up.

'What do you know?' I asked Stride. It was about time I heard his side of the story. All the mystery surrounding him was beginning to aggravate me.
Blaze got up from the sofa; luckily, he escaped with a few minor scratches. I could not tell what he must have been thinking. Poor guy though, I thought, as I saw him limp over to Stride's file cabinet with blood trickling down his face. If I had seen what I turned into, I probably would have reacted in the same way.

'I need a bottle, is that okay?' he said nonchantly.

'Sure, but don't try to leave now...'

'Leave? You must be fucking joking. If there are vampires in here, I dread to think what the fuck is out there?' he said, pointing towards the door.

Stride sat deep in thought for a while. I didn't think this would've been too difficult for him but looking at him sat there, there seemed to be a lot more going on with him than I initially thought, but nothing could've shocked me more than what he was about to tell me.

'Jyrki, you know how you think you are the last? Well, that isn't entirely true.'

I gasped. Blaze thumped the bottle down on the cabinet.

'What?' We both said simultaneously.

'Yes, there is, and he has been helping me. You see, I've been looking for you or the past 40 years.'

I was dumbstruck by his revelation. It wasn't at all what I was expecting to hear from him. I assumed maybe he was a little crazy, perhaps a mental asylum patient gone AWOL, but he really did take me by surprise. I sat on the edge of my seat waiting for him to unravel his story.

'So, who is he? I've been feeling like I have been followed and just earlier I thought I saw someone outside the studios...was that him?'

'For everyone's protection right now, I can't say who he is, and yes I've sent him to keep an eye on you. These Secret Order people or whatever only knows you are here, apart from us and one other, we are the only ones who know of his existence, and in fact we are the only ones who know of the existence of Vampires.'

'Another vampire?' Blaze wiped the sweat from his forehead and took another swig of the bottle.

For the first time since I saw everyone disintegrate into ash before me, I felt a sense of peace within me. Yet, in my mind, I didn't know how this could've been possible. There was nobody left, for which I was absolutely certain. My clan was the only race of vampires in existence. I could feel the rush of excitement run through my veins, as I waited for Stride to unfold his story.

Stride sat back against the chair and took another sip from the bottle he was holding.

'My father was in the Korean war, when his best friend got shot by a sniper. Up until the day he died when I was seventeen, he was adamant that what he saw on that fateful night was the God's honest truth. He watched this human-like creature drag the body through a hedge. He called out to him but he scarpered. My father chased after him and found his friend with two bite marks on his neck; his blood was almost completely drained. Beside his body he found a piece of brown parchment that the creature must've dropped.'

'So, hang on there a moment, this vampire obviously cannot walk in daylight? How has he survived? Where is he now?'

'He survived in the underground. He traced me about a year ago, wanting the parchment back, but I had already done a lot of research and so I offered to help him, not fully realising what he was at the time...'

'What was in the parchment?'

'It was the prophecy, written in an Ancient Egyptian language.'

CHAPTER SEVENTEEN

I heard Blazes mobile ringing in the distance, just outside of my own thoughts on the news that the ancient prophecy had been found. I heard talk of 'I'm coming now,' and 'murder weapon,' swim into my own stream of consciousness. I turned to Blaze, who still looked very much on edge, holding the mobile phone a few inches from his ear staring into oblivion.

I shot up from the floor as I could sense the instilled panic and fear that surrounded him. Having forgotten about my own revelation just earlier, my move wasn't very tactful. Blaze flinched as I approached him. I stood only inches away from him. He made me feel like a predator after its prey. I saw the pain in his eyes. He began to sweat profusely and his breathing became heavier. He looked as though he wanted to say something to me, but instead he turned to Stride who was stood next to me looking at him inquisitively.

'What's the matter with him now? Stride asked me. 'Boy, you may aswell accept it now, he is a vampire and yes, he almost killed you, but, and what I'm gonna say is important, he didn't so get over it and tell us what is going on with you?'

'Do you have to be that harsh?' I said to Stride. 'He's obviously had a shock tonight can't you be a little more sympathetic? You've had forty years to get used to this.'

Blaze shook his head. 'April,' he sucked in a ragged breath and a look of dread melted across his face.

'What's wrong with April?'

'What has a month of the year gotta do with this?' Stride asked.

Blaze flew into a rage. 'It's my sister you fucking moron,' he yelled.

'Ok Blaze chill, tell us what has happened? Is she okay?'

'What do you care huh?' he spat.

I did care, perhaps a little too much than I should.

'She's been taken hostage and I bet it's all your fucking fault,' he said breaking down into a heap on the floor.

Somehow I knew where all this was going.

'Has this got anything to do with Dr. Matthews's murder?'

'She was at the museum earlier, sorting out Dr. Matthews's office when some Egyptian men took her. She's locked in a hotel in the city somewhere,' he said. 'They better not lay a finger on her she's all the family I have.'

He looked at me begging me to help him whilst still undecided about whether he could trust me.

'Why would they want your sister?' Stride asked.

'She's the curator of the museum; she was the one who organised that bloody Egyptian exhibition.'

'Oh this is getting interesting,' Stride nodded.

'Did she say what hotel?' I asked him.

'No, her mobile cut off.'

'Stride, do you have the prophecy on you?'

'Er, no, the other guy has it.'

I had to take a minute. So far this evening was in the running for being the worst night I've had since I arrived in New York.

'I'm just going out a minute, I need to think.'

I leaned against the doorframe of the warehouse watching the rain beat down into the puddle by my feet, when I sensed something was standing around the corner of the building. It was the same feeling I had in Finland when I sensed the 'Others.' I didn't want to alarm Blaze and Stride, so I looked back to check that they wouldn't notice me gone. Stride was talking to Blaze on the sofa with their backs turned to me.

'Jyrki?'

'Huh?' I looked around me not sure of what I was expecting to see; until the voice called me again and I realised it was the same voice I had in my head from Finland.

'What do you want?' I whispered as I edged slowly around the building.

'You should go to the museum.'

'What? What are you talking about?' I whispered back.

'The answers are in the museum.'

'Right, I've had enough, who are you?' I demanded.

I wasn't prepared to wait for an answer after all I have waited too long for this moment. Curiosity was surely gnawing away at me as I could see its shadow stretched out on the floor. Just one more step, one more step I thought to finally solving this mystery. I gripped the edge of the building and quickly snatched a glimpse behind.

'Oh shit!'

I pulled back instantly unable to believe what I saw.

At the corner of my eye, I could see the shadow moving towards me.

'Did I just see right?'

'Yes, you saw right.'

I glanced down then back up again, unable to believe what I had just saw. A large black wolf stood peering up at me with its green eyes that illuminated in the darkness.

'You're the others, wolves?' I spluttered. 'This has to be a fucking joke right?'

The creature didn't move its mouth still, but preferred to communicate with me telepathically.

'Yes, we're wolves and we're also the guardians of the ancient secrets,' he said, walking around me. 'Don't act so surprised by the mere fact that I am a wolf, we aren't your enemies you know despite what you may have been led to believe.'

'You're the guardians? So that would mean Jafar is one of you too?'

'Yes. Well, he was until he was lured into the underworld.'

'Underworld? What can you tell me? I need some help as Blaze's sister has been kidnapped.'

'I shall meet with you later. For now just take my advice and go to the museum. Something awaits you there.'

'Jyrki! Where the fuck are ya?' Stride yelled.

'Go now, you must go back indoors and not mention us to anyone yet.'

I couldn't believe it, all this time and they were wolves. I was expecting a lot worse or was I underestimating them.

'Maybe we should go to the museum, check things out?' I said, 'Do you have any four wheel transportation?'

'Sure, my van is out the back. I'll get my keys. Er, any particular reason?'

'Just trust me on this.'

I looked at Blaze who was sitting on the sofa. 'You can trust me y'know,' I didn't expect forgiveness right away, I just wanted him to know he could still trust me and despite the demon, my curse, I was still the same Jyrki he had met at the bar.

84

He looked up at me with a little less hatred and nodded.

'We need to work together ok, these people have something we both need.'

'Sure, just can't quite believe it y'know...' he said, unable to look me in the eye.

'I know, and I'm still very sorry about this. I never wanted you to see me like that.'

'Yeah,' he scoffed. 'You and me both, man. You're fucking scary. Remind me not to get on the wrong side of you!'

I smirked. 'It's gonna take a while to get used to, but hopefully when this prophecy has been found, I'll be able to break this curse once and for all.'

'Come on you two,' Stride yelled from the van, 'there's an ancient prophecy to be found.'

'Yeah and my sister,' Blaze muttered as he walked out of the warehouse.

CHAPTER EIGHTEEN

'Bloody weather!' Stride tutted as he switched on the windscreen wipers.

I had to agree, it hadn't really stopped raining since I arrived in New York over a week ago.

The conversation in the van was becoming a bit stale since Blaze had found out I was a vampire. For the last ten minutes, we sat staring out of the window watching the museum for any sign of trouble.

'So what are we doing here?' Blaze asked.

I must've nudged him with my elbow as I shrugged because he flinched and edged towards the van door away from me.

'Yeah, what are we doing here?' Stride asked.

'I just have a feeling we should be here.'

'I don't know what you're hoping to find mind you, the book has gone.'

'Hey Stride, where's your enthusiasm gone? We've got to start somewhere and besides when were you planning on introducing me to the other guy?'

'Soon, as soon as he has finished putting false tracks down for you. We can't let on that there are two of you.'

'Why?'

'Well, didn't you ever read the first part of the prophecy?'

'No, I can't read Egyptian. My father wouldn't tell me much either, whether it was because he couldn't or what, I don't know.'

'Well, according the Secret Order, you my friend are the last vampire, so whoever was sent to kill you all that day, either, didn't realise this vampire was still alive, or they knew. My guess is they didn't.'

'Right, so this is why he has been keeping low. So he can help when the time comes to end this curse?'

'Yep, so if we had the second part, we'd know what we're meant to do. I'm just getting so pissing annoyed now that it's taking so long.'

'There's a second part?' Blaze asked.

'Yes, it's an ancient prophecy, oh long story, but the Book of The Dead was supposed to contain it, but that has been stolen now and we haven't a fucking clue where to start looking.'

'Oh that book. I remember April had a strange call the other week saying she could have it loan for her exhibit. She said the call was totally unexpected.'

I looked at Stride. 'Are you thinking what I'm thinking?'

'What? What you're talking about?' Blaze panicked.

'I think that's why they have April,' I said, 'they must have the second part already and if April can decipher it for them...oh shit.'

I slammed my fist down on the dashboard, startling Blaze sat next to me.

'Do you think she's alright? They won't harm her will they?' Blaze said.

'No, no, just calm down, ok, let's do what we've come here to do first. So come on Jyrki, what the fuck are we doing here?'

'Just wait a bit longer, I have a feeling something will show up anytime soon.'

'What are you now, a psychic vampire?' Blaze said.

'Not quite. Although, my instinct is much better developed than yours.'

Blaze sighed and tried to relax a bit, but his insistence on tapping the dashboard to whatever song he had playing in his head was pissing me off.

'So Stride, how did you become involved in all this then?' Blaze asked obviously trying to take his mind off things.

'Ah, well lad I'll tell you. If you want that is? It all began with my father, as you know. When I saw the prophecy as a young lad it fascinated me so much I read everything I could on demonology and Ancient Egypt. I can even picture my dad talking to me about it now. No one ever believed him thankfully.'

'But you kept researching, why?'

'Of course I did. I was in a biker bar in Wales one night talking to this lad. Well you know after a few drinks everyone looks the same, yeah? Well, you know me, and my big mouth; I started yapping about the prophecy to this guy. He reminded me of the great Brandon Lee, you know of him don't you?' He said as he looked at me, 'Oh maybe not, well, he was extremely interested in all this shit I was spouting off about vampires and the end of the world. In fact, he was too interested and that should've been a sign for me to shut up. Well, it must've been about closing time and the most of the punters had gone home. I was sat in the corner of the pub talking to him and the next thing I know he asks if my father was in Korea. I almost crapped myself. Since then I've been helping him to find you. You're not much of trackers are you for a bunch of animals? Took him sodding years to find my dad but he ends up finding me instead...' he laughed, 'In a little town called the Mumbles.'

'For real? So why are you here now, in New York?'

'Well lad this is where it's all going down innit? We managed to decipher that much.'

'Sorry to butt in but how is all this supposed to be helping me find my sister? Don't you think we should call the police?'

'Noooo!' We both yelled.

'There's no sense getting the law involved, the next thing you know it will be the government and then the media and before you know it we'll have panic in the streets, so no, absolutely not, we can do this our way, and if the worst comes to the worst, I call my mate Jimmy,' Stride said.

I glanced at Stride 'Jimmy?'

'Jimmy Wolffskin, my mate who works in the FBI, and believe me we can trust him, ok.'

The man never ceases to amaze me. Just when I think I am getting to know him, he tells me something else to make me nervous. I didn't bother questioning him any further. I wanted to check out the museum before dawn.

'Perhaps we should go and take a look.' I suggested.

Blaze shook his head. 'You can count me out.'

I gave him a stern look.

'Well you're the vampire, you go first.'

'Right, okay then I will. Stride?'

'Nah, I'm staying here incase we need a quick getaway.'

'Are you sure about this? I mean, the Ankh giving you psychic messages or something, it sounds kinda fucked up?' Blaze asked

'Two days ago, you didn't believe vampires were real.' I laughed.

'Okay, point taken. Here, do you want my mobile...er, just incase?'

'Your mobile?'

'Yeah, it's a phone for fuck sake. You know what that is surely?'

I took the mobile from Blaze and jumped out of the van. As I slammed the door, I overheard Blaze remark to Stride, 'I hope he knows how to use it.' I didn't. Twenty first century technology was beyond me.

I ran over the road towards the main doors of the building. It looked empty, apart from a few security lights outside the door. I turned back towards the van and shrugged. There didn't appear to be anyone here, maybe my hunch was wrong.

CHAPTER NINETEEN

The sound of my boots squelching was driving me insane as I walked up the steps to the museum door. I was soaked, agitated and hungry. If anything dared cross my path right now, it wouldn't last for very long. I tried pushing the main doors but they were locked and didn't look like they have been tampered with either. So what was I meant to be doing here? April wasn't far from my mind either. I couldn't let onto to Blaze that I had feelings for her as I somehow gathered he wouldn't be too happy with his sister dating a vampire.

'Damn!' I shouted as I tripped over an oversized plant pot beside the pillars. That'll teach me for allowing my mind to stray. I lifted myself up and pushed my hair away from my face when I heard Blaze's mobile going off in my pocket. 'Shit!' I cursed. I stared blankly at this peculiar looking device. I knew I had to press something. But what? It cut off and rang again. After the third attempt I was getting rather frustrated and felt like throwing the damn thing, but luckily my finger must've slipped on the answer button just as I was about to sling it. I heard Blaze's voice on the other end. He sounded to me as if he was scared.

I held the phone to my ear. 'What is it?' I asked. I did feel like an idiot talking to a piece of plastic, but hey, I thought, you can't fault these humans, they were pretty intelligent.

'Come 'round the back now,' Blaze rasped.

Bloody hell! What the fuck is Blaze up to now. I was hoping he'd stay out of trouble but I knew that was unlikely with Stride about.

I dropped the phone and ran around the side of the building. The loading entrance door was open ajar, which meant the security alarms had been cut. I looked at it and began to feel nervous at what I might find behind it, but as I was feeling weak anyway; I decided to let the vampire overtake my body. I couldn't go in there unprepared, and it was best to have that extra strength. I already had a sufficient amount of blood earlier, so I knew I wouldn't go for any humans tonight.

The musty smell of the interior didn't agree with me. I walked past the stairway that was illuminated by the moonlight shining through the window at the top. In front of me an arch doorway that led into the new Egyptian exhibit. I acted on my instinct and walked through.

All was calm in the room. Not a thing was out of place either. I jumped over the yellow security tape the police had put around the empty glass cabinet, which I guessed once held the Book of The Dead. I gave it a quick inspection until my ears became alerted to the sound of Blaze whimpering in the corner behind me.

'Man, what are you doing here?' I whispered. 'I thought you was staying with Stride in the van...um, where is Stride anyway?' I said as I looked around the room.

'I had to come and warn you there was someone following you, but, but he got to me first,' he said sucking in a sharp breath.

'Okay, just chill, who was he and where is he now?'

'He looked like you. I thought it was you, but then I realised it couldn't have been you because he was following you in here...Jyrki, he looked like that guy down the docks that night!'

'Blaze! Listen to me ok, calm down now, alright. You did the right thing.'

'I'm only doing this for April you got that. I still haven't forgiven you for lying to me.'

'I know; I understand perfectly.'

Blazes' facial expression change, he looked twice as fearful as he did when he saw me shift into a vampire at the warehouse earlier. I followed the swift flow of movement from his eyes. He tried to talk but it was if his mouth had become paralysed with fear. I could sense someone was standing behind me and it wasn't human.

Slowly, I got up from the floor and turned around, terrified of the thought of what was going to greet me, when the touch of moonlight seeping from the window articulated the features on the face that stood before me. I looked at him and gasped. The familiar deep-set blue eyes that last saw me so many years ago at the compound were now looking at me again. This wasn't possible I kept thinking. I reached out my hand to touch him, to feel that he was indeed real and not just another dark memory from home. I saw in his eyes a sudden relief of all his pain as he realised it was really me.

'Jyrki...it's really you?'

'Draven! How…this isn't possible?'

'Yes, it is,' he said, clenching my arms. 'You have no idea how good it is to see you again.'

This can't be happening to me. All those years alone and now…now, for the first time I felt complete again. I struggled to get the words out that were in my head but instead I just looked at him, thankful to be in his presence once more. How I longed to hear my native language one more time. To have it spoken to me by my brother again was something I never thought possible.

'How… I don't understand?'

He looked haggard and worn. His shoulder length dark hair looked greasy and fell over his tired face. Although it wasn't very surprising considering he survived in the underground for so long. He smiled at me and threw his arms around my neck. It was so good to have my brother back.

'This is unbelievable. I thought you all perished that day. Is father here too?'

The mention of father pained him deeply; it wasn't so hard to see. He raised a hand to his forehead, rubbing it as if to relieve all the tension and worry that has plagued him for years.

'No, he isn't. I don't really know what happened to them all, do you?' I did, but I wasn't up to talking about this right now.

'Human?' He nodded to Blaze.

'Oh Blaze,' relieved he had changed the subject. 'Draven this is Blaze, but I see you've already met.'

Draven peered over my shoulder; his eyes glinted of mischief as he flashed a smirk at Blaze who was still crouched into the corner by the door.

'Yes, I thought he was some Egyptian or worse until I smelt his blood,' Draven laughed. 'I gave you a fright though, didn't I. Down the docks that night?' he grinned.

'It's okay Blaze, Draven is my brother. What were you doing down the docks anyway? Have you been following me too?'

'Yes, Stride wanted me to keep an eye on you. So many times, I had wanted to say something to you but I couldn't. It was such a relief to find out you was still alive. Until I met Stride that night I didn't even know where to begin looking for you.'

'He did say. So you lost the prophecy?'

Draven lowered his head in shame.

'I've travelled the world in the last century trying to track you down. I believed you to be still alive, I had to, you were the only thing that kept me going, but I must admit there were times when things got too much and I did many stupid things. Things I truly regret. I was in Korea for a short while, when I almost, almost Jyrki, drained this one guy who was between life and death. Imagine if I had sired another vampire. Can you imagine what would have happened? Anyway, I lost the prophecy that night and as fate would have it, Stride's father had picked it up and thankfully kept it a secret all these years.'

Blaze got up from the floor and adjusted his jacket; he looked uncomfortable and unsure with what to do with himself.

'I, er...well, um, two vampires huh? Who would've thought it? You know what guys? I'm not going to even bother trying to get my head around this, it's too fucking mind-blowing.'

In the ensuing darkness, I could hear the faint tapping of feet walking along the vinyl flooring out in the hallway. I shifted my gaze from Blaze to the door and in walked Stride clutching a pile of paper.

'Good idea lad, it's the best way to be honest. Ignorance is always bliss, but remember it could also you cost you your life.'

'Stride? Why didn't you say it was Draven you found that night huh?' He cocked a cheeky smile and winked. 'I couldn't, I didn't want to give names incase the you know who's happened to be hanging around, but anyway I just came across some papers in Dr. Matthew's office, can you make any sense out of them?'

'Give them 'ere,' Draven said. 'Looks like it's an early form of the Ancient Egyptian language?'

'Can you read it?' he asked.

'It's not something I've got around to learning to be honest.'

'Let me take a look.' Blaze walked nervously over toward Draven and reluctantly took the papers from him. After looking them over for a few seconds, he spoke.

'Hm, I may be wrong, but April had stuff like this. If we can find her I'm sure she will decipher these for you.'

'You know someone who could decipher these, really? So who's your sister? Is she the woman who works here? If it is she was taken to the

Grand hotel yesterday by some Arab men.'

'Well what are we standing here for then? C'mon let's go,' Blaze said.

'Blaze, storming into there right now will make matters worse. We'll go back Stride's place,' I said, 'and come up with a plan.'

'Sorry to disappoint, but no can do. Just got a text from Jimmy, the police have raided my place. Seems like our foreign Egyptian friends have alerted the authorities and said I have abducted April.'

'You're fucking kidding? Who would do a thing like that?' Blaze stammered.

'I know who and he's not all he seems either.'

We all turned around sharply towards the door and gasped at the wolf walking casually over to us.

'What the fuck is that? A dog?' Stride yelled.

'I wanna know why it's talking in my head?' Blaze blurted out.

'Fear me not my friends my name is Randulphr, protector of the ancient secrets.'

'What are you doing here?'

'You know it?' Draven asked me so surprisingly.

'We met earlier, outside Stride's place.'

'Jafar, or to you my friend,' he looked at Stride. 'Jimmy is not to be trusted. He is after the Ankh for himself. He betrayed us when the protection shield was broken at the compound. Mardok sent us to save you but we were too late. Another vampire, a half breed is on the loose, he is working with him.'

'A half breed you say?' Draven said.

'Yes that's right, there is another.'

We all went silent for a while. Stride stroked his white beard and stood beside Draven, thinking things through as he normally does. Part of me wasn't so shocked to hear about a half breed having just found out about Draven, but nonetheless it wasn't a good thing to hear right now. 'So you did not kill my family?' I asked.

'No, never. We trusted Amroath, but unfortunately one of you did break the agreement.'

'And Jimmy is what?' Stride asked. 'Not that I particularly want to hear it.'

'He's one of the hounds of the apocalypse.'

'You mean he's a fucking wolf?' Stride said. 'That can't be fucking right, I've known him too long. Don't you think I would've found out?'

I stood contently beside the window in Blaze's apartment watching the new dawn rising over the city. I reveled in the burnt orange glow that tainted the darkness behind it. I longed to be a part of that world, where the darkness and light met in one continuous flow of energy. I gave a hopeful smile and drew the curtain shut tightly.

'We're going to need to talk Jyrki.'

I turned to look at Draven sitting on the leather chair at the far corner of the room. He poured another sachet of blood into a cup and sat back against the seat. I was feeling much happier since I discovered he was alive and now I was ready to hear the truth of what happened that day, no matter how painful.

Blaze was stretched out on the sofa strumming on his acoustic. He looked as if he had a lot weighing on his mind.

'Where's Randulphr gone?' he asked, still strumming on the guitar.

'Back to keep an eye on Jimmy,' Draven said as he took a sip from a cup.

'Anyone want a glass of this fine Scotch? Stride said holding up a half drank bottle. 'Nope? Then I take it's all mine then.'

'Jyrki, sit down, we must talk.'

I sat down on the sofa opposite him and switched the lamp on.

'Father told me a few hours before everyone what was happening. That's why I ran to you from the lake when I heard all the commotion going on. The day before all this was due to take place he had word from a guy called Mardok.'

'Mardok? I've heard that name before. Father spoke of him once.'

'Yes, he was an aide to Pharaoh Ramesses. Apparently, as far as I know he helped Father escape from Egypt.'

'So you must know who killed our clan? You were there Draven. How did you even survive?'

Draven lowered his head; he couldn't bear to look at me. 'I cannot quite remember. I was knocked unconscious and dumped into a cave on the mountains not long after you left. I assumed whoever had killed our family, had killed you too. But, Jyrki there's something I must tell you as I've a feeling this will affect the prophecy and everything else. I feel ashamed, not for what I did, but for what it has caused.'

He paused for a few moments and turned his gaze towards the window. 'You see Jyrki, I fell in love with a woman from the village. I shouldn't have let it happen, I know, but...'

'What were you doing there anyway, you knew the rules?'

'You should know better than anyone that it was never easy being alone for days on ends, with no companionship, no female company. Well, everything just got to me one night and I decided to leave the compound. I had just gone for a walk this particular night when a couple of fisherman saw me and offered me a ride back to the main island. It was there I saw a woman tending to her horse, I stopped and began a conversation, I don't know what made me do it, I guess I was just curious. She was beautiful and didn't seem to mind what I was, which fascinated me even more. Honestly Jyrki, I didn't think one trip out of that place would cause so much trouble.'

'Who was she and did father know?'

'No, father didn't know at the time. Her name was Clara, she had the most beautiful long raven hair, and big blue eyes,' he said. 'I guess we were found out as I had left the safe zone once too often and no I did not change her. So, you see, Father's blood is on my hands. I killed them Jyrki, don't you see? All this is entirely my fault.'

He sat upright on the chair and took another sip from the cup before rubbing his forehead. His eyes were bloodshot and his once youthful good looks had now taken a beating with all the guilt he had carried.

I was stunned. 'You were with a human, a female human? Damn it Draven, it's no wonder the agreement was broken. How could you be so fucking selfish?'

'You can't make me feel any worse than I already do. If I could've controlled myself better then I guess none of this would've happened, but it has, so now we have to find a way of resolving this.'

'But you lost Jyrki?' Stride asked. 'Couldn't you sense him? Track him even?'

'No, the others must've been protecting him too. But as you know Stride, I have been searching for him for years, and it wasn't until I managed to decipher part of the prophecy that I realised that you, Jyrki, was going to end up here, in New York at the same time the book was going to be here. It is written in the prophecy, everything we need to

know about who we are, where we come from. I only hope we find something in there that will help rid us of this disgusting curse.'
Draven handed me the first part of the prophecy. I looked at the parchment. Written in burnt red ink were several lines of text in hierlyglyphics, a very old language that neither of us could really decipher.

'It looks as though pieces are missing?'

'You're right, which brings us back to the papers that Stride found earlier. Dr. Matthews had copied them from the prophecy just before he was murdered. It was April who discovered the parchment in the book upon its arrival. I just only hope April hasn't managed to decipher it yet, not to that lot anyway.'

'Well, from what I can gather from this piece of the prophecy it says something along the lines of, 'the return of the chosen one.'

'Return? That would mean you Jyrki? But where the hell are you returning to?' Stride asked.
Draven got up from his seat and took the parchment from my hands.

'It does too. I can't believe I missed that.'

'Then we're going to have to find out and soon.'

CHAPTER TWENTY-ONE

I couldn't listen to anymore of this talk on prophecies. The mere fact
that I was about to leave for somewhere unknown disturbed me greatly.
I got up from the sofa and walked into the kitchen, leaving Blaze and
Draven talking amongst themselves.
   'Stride did you fetch us some blood?'
   'Aye, it's in the fridge,' he said as he poured himself a coffee.
   'Fridge! My fridge?' Blaze yelled from the living room.
   'Well yeah I don't have one in the back of the car like,' Stride laughed
Just as I was about to open the fridge door Blaze came running in with
a disgusted look on his face.
   'Is it human blood? It had better not be. I have left over curry in there
I was planning to having later.'
Stride smirked at me and then took a sip of his coffee. Even I didn't
know whose blood it was which was slightly off putting.
   'Hell no lad, they gave that up, isn't that right Jyrki?'
I held the sachet of blood in my hands wondering whether I should
drink it or not. Knowing Stride I didn't really want to ask where it had
come from.
   'Of course,' I said to Blaze. Although he didn't really look convinced.
'It's cool, honestly; I haven't touched human blood for a very long
time. In fact I am over it, to an extent.'
   'What do you mean by that? Fucking hell man, you mean to say you
have murdered people for their blood?'
That question hit a nerve with me. I didn't really know what to say to
him.
   'Blaze, just relax for fuck sake,' Stride said, lighting up a cigarette.
Draven walked in the kitchen wondering what the hell was going on.
   'What's wrong Blaze? You look like you've seen a ghost?'
   'What's wrong with me? You wanna know what's wrong with me,
well I'll tell ya. He has lived with me for the past fortnight but
somehow it slips his mind to tell me that he has murdered people to
drink their blood. Now you fucking tell me what's wrong with that!'
I didn't feel like drinking the blood anymore so I threw it into the waste
bin.

'Blaze, we are vampires what else do you expect us to drink?' Draven said.

'Look, if it's any consolation we weren't to drink human blood. Our father had made an agreement with Mardok, that in return for his life he would not drink from a human so that we would never expose our identity. But, of course some things cannot be helped. It's like nature. You can't stop a cat from chasing and eating birds can you? Well the same applies to us. It is in our nature, our genetic make-up.'

'It's cannibalism, that what that is, not nature.'

'Yeah, you are quite right, but we didn't ask for this, you must understand that.'

Blaze nodded.

'Yeah, I guess you're right. I don't think of you as a…meat eater. Not now, since I've lived with you for a while. So your secret trips out at night weren't you meeting some lady friend then?'

I smirked. I only wish it had been.

'Nope, I was too busy stopping myself from draining you while you slept. No, I'm just joking. I felt uncomfortable about staying here since you didn't really know what I was. So, I was drinking twice the amount of blood to reassure myself I wouldn't attack you.'

'Oh jeez, thanks,' Blaze laughed. 'So, er this curse you mentioned then, how did it come about?'

'Shall we go and sit down first?' I said and walked back into the living room.

I sat on the sofa and rested my legs on the coffee table. Draven stayed in the kitchen.

'Well, the curse as I call it was passed down from my father. My mother was a human.'

'Shit really?'

'Yeah, I have a mother. Don't looked so shocked. Her name was Katariina. Father met her when he first arrived in Finland a hundred and twenty three years ago. He was with the last of the New Bloods clan, who were friends of father's from Egypt. As the story goes, he met her by the lake one evening. She was crying as she had missed the boat to the mainland. Father told me he did not want to get involved with her troubles but the woman noticed him and begged him to help her. At the time father was still struggling with his inner demon and snapped when he smelt that she was human. Once she had seen him change, he had no choice but to protect the clan and change her. He did not want to kill her. He said, she was the most beautiful thing he had ever seen and knew at once when he changed her the demon would not last ten years at least. Well, after that he vowed never to kill another human again, and he never. That is also why I am not a half-blood, my mother was changed.'

Blaze looked at me inquisitively.

'So how old are you then?'

'I'm a hundred and nineteen. The demon keeps us young enough to slay, but I suppose we will age to whatever age is appropriate for us to live comfortably at. I could stay looking as if I'm in my thirties for another hundred years. It depends. If I can get rid of the curse I will become mortal, a human being just like you, because that is essentially what I really am. The first vampires, like my father were humans. Many of them were killed in Egypt when the sun came up. They did not know that daylight could kill them.'

'Why did they not know?'

'Well, nobody really knew of the curse except a select few. It was a dangerous thing to unleash on the world, and that's why it has been hidden for thousands if not millions of years. The spell came from a very special edition of the Book of the Dead, so light being the opposite would banish the darkness.'

'And what about the Ankh, that allows you to walk in daylight, right?'

'Yes. I am not aware of its history but the reason I have it is because, father overheard Mardok arguing with Jafar one day in the temple. He wanted the Ankh but Mardok would not tell him where it was. The Ankh is a very important symbol. It is the universal giver of life. Whoever has it, it would give them the power they desire. Obviously, ours were to walk in sunlight. However, before Mardok trusted my father with the Ankh, he was shown the ancient prophecy. On reading it, he vowed to protect it and return it when the deed has been done.'

'Deed?'

'Well, Stride mentioned something about trying to stop an apocalypse.'

'Oh for fuck sake, I don't think I want to hear anymore.'

'I know what you mean. I never really understood why Father never spoke about what he read in the prophecy though.'

'Perhaps there was something a little too close to home in it?'

'What do you mean?'

'What I mean is, maybe he read something that concerned you or Draven and he did not wish to talk about it. Or maybe there was something about him written in there.'

Stride walked into the room. He obviously overheard our whole conversation.

'Did you ever think he was at risk of jeopardising his position if he was to talk about any of the contents before its time?'

'Yeah, I see what you mean. Although it doesn't make any of this easier to deal with. I still have the worry of not knowing where I am going.'

CHAPTER TWENTY-TWO

The tension was beginning to show in us all, especially in Blaze who was now pacing about the living room. He was unshaven and had been wearing the same Guns N Roses t-shirt for the last few days. I had to get him out of here before he would lose it completely.

'Blaze, do you want to go and get something to eat? There's not much we can do here at the minute.'

'Huh?' he said. 'Er, yeah I guess I could do with some air. But what about what Draven has found out, what if you're in some sort of danger?'

'I think I'm capable enough of handling whatever it is. Hey Draven, we're just going out for a bit, if you need us ask Stride to call Blaze on the mobile.'

'Sure, I'm just going over some of April's books anyway. Not much else to do,' he said looking up from the book he was holding.

'Looks like he has the right idea eh?' Blaze laughed, pointing at Stride.

Stride was half asleep on the sofa clutching an empty bottle of Scotch. I tutted and shook my head at him as I walked out the door.

'Oi, here's your sunglasses, Jyrki. You don't wanna strain those eyes with the sun now do you?' Blaze said, handing me my sunglasses.

'I guess not, we'll go to Danny's Diner a few blocks away, yeah? I reckon it'll do me good to try your human food for a change. I quite fancy trying some cheesecake.' I was only trying to crack a joke to ease Blaze's dark mood. Judging by his beaming smile under the freshly grown beard, it seemed too had done the trick.

Blaze narrowed his eyes and grinned. 'You are going to eat cheesecake? With what? Strawberry preserve, the vampire kind?' he laughed.

'Now, don't tempt me,' I said in all seriousness. I saw him flick me a worried look. 'I'm joking, ok.'

The sounds of the city this early in the morning was actually a breath of fresh air as we walked from Blaze's apartment through the streets of downtown Manhattan. The steam rising from the grates and the passing of the yellow cabs was now a familiar sight to me; it was as if I had adopted this place as my second home.

'So what do you think is going to happen?'

I shrugged and continued walking with my hands in my pocket. 'I don't know. Anything is possible.'

'Anything is possible?' That's right, vampires and wolves running around the city and nobody but us is any wiser. It just doesn't seem right does it?'

'Nope, it doesn't, but it's a good thing,' I said looking at a bunch of kids walking past on their way to school. 'I wouldn't like to see the innocent get hurt.'

I could smell the freshly made coffee lilting in the air and the sound of Elvis Presley coming from the door. It certainly smelt better than the dreaded blood I had to force down my neck every day.

'Here?' Blaze asked. He pointed to an old firehouse, which had been reformed into a 1950's diner.

'Yeah this is the place.'

We walked in through the double doors and was greeted by the smile of an overly keen blonde waitress in a tight fitting red and white uniform.

'Table for two?' She smiled as she walked us over to the corner booth at the back of the room.

Blaze sat down opposite me on their red leather seats by the window. I glanced around at the 1950's decor when my eyes caught sight of a retro poster hanging just above his head.

'All customers with serious personal problems will be served first.' I smirked. Blaze glanced up and looked at me oddly.

'What? What's so funny?'

'Never mind,' I said, still trying to contain myself.

'Here's the menus, just give me a holler when you're ready to order. Oops sorry,' she said as she dropped the menus on the floor.

'Do you want a hand?' Blaze grinned.

I couldn't keep my eyes off her cleavage as she deliberately bent down to pick up the menu she had dropped.

'Here you go. I'll be back to take your order when you're ready,' she smiled as she walked back to the counter.

'I think she has the hot's for you,' Blaze sniggered. 'What's your secret man? Whatever it is, can I have some?' he said as his eyes followed her about the room.

I shook my head, slightly embarrassed by it all. 'Whatever I have, you really don't want mate. I can assure you,' I said fiddling about with the ketchup bottle.

'Yeah, but aren't you vampires supposed to be really attractive to the opposite sex or something?'

'Well, yeah. When we turn on the charm,' I grinned

'So what are you having? I don't want to be long incase something happens.'

'Just a slice of cheesecake will do and I'll try a hot chocolate,' I said, still reading the menu.

'Wow, you're going all out today aren't you? I wonder what the Count would say if he saw you eating this shit?' he laughed, he'd probably defang you!'

'I'm trying to be as human as possible.'

'Yeah,' he nodded towards the blonde waitress. 'I think that one prefers you as you are.'

I snatched a sneaky side-glance at the woman wiping the counter top down. As she saw me looking, she turned away. It was becoming quite an annoying game with Blaze now, but at least it was easing the stress of what tonight would bring.

'Err miss;' he said snapping his fingers, 'we're ready to order. So,' he said, turning to me, 'did you know about these wolves?'

'No I didn't. I sensed an animal watching me back in Finland but I couldn't quite connect with their breed...'

'You've seen them before?'

'Not seen, but they've spoken to me.'

Blaze was about to ask me something else, when he was interrupted by the waitress.

'So guys what are you ordering?'

'Err, just a black coffee for me and a hot chocolate and some pancakes for him.'

He was still sniggering and I'm sure the waitress caught on, as her face went as red as the blood in her veins.

Blaze grinned at me and I had a sneaky suspicion what he was about to do.

'What's your name doll?'

'Jules. Why, who's asking?'

I turned to look out of the window.

'My mate just there?' he said, pointing a finger at me.

'Well that's a shame because I thought you were. Anyway, I'll get your order,' she winked at him.

I covered my mouth with my hand to hide my smirk from Blaze. Blaze looked dumbstruck.

'Did she really say me? Fucking hell. I'd better ask her for her number. Too late my friend,' he grinned.

I was somewhat relieved anyway as I already had my eye on April.

'There you go, enjoy,' she put the drinks on the table and handed Blaze the receipt.

'Thank you,' he said staring at her.

'No problem, all part of the service,' she said smiling.

Blaze looked down at the receipt and smiled.

'She left her number on here.'

'Did she, well she must be desperate.' I joked. Hey, isn't that your mobile I can hear?' I said.

'Oh fuck yeah,' he said, putting his coffee down.

'Hello? Who's this? Hang on I'll put Jyrki on.'

'Who is it?'

'Draven.'

'Hi, what's up? You're serious? Well tell him to stay put until we get back.'

I could tell by the sound of his voice that something was wrong. I listened to what he had to say before relaying it all back to Blaze.

'Er, Stride had a call from Jimmy,' I said

'The wolf?'

'Yes, the wolf. He wants to meet him later,' I shrugged

'Why? But hold on, how is he human anyway, does he transform when there's a full moon or what?'

'I have no idea why he is in human form or what his game is; in fact I don't trust him at all. I'd better go with Stride, are you coming?'

'Of course,' he said as he gulped down the remainder of his coffee. 'That bastard has my sister. Anyway, what does he want to see Stride for?'

'He wants to come to some sort of an arrangement.'

'Yeah right,' Blaze scoffed then realised that I wasn't joking. His expression hardened. 'I'll arrange him if he touches her. Come on, let's get out of here.'

'What time is it?'

'Going on for eleven,' I said, turning back to look through the café window.

'Do you think April is ok?'

'Of course she is, now don't worry.'

'I know a shortcut back, just through that alleyway across the road.'

Blaze was chatting away about having Jules' number when he noticed I wasn't paying him anymore attention.

'Hey, did you hear anything I just said?'

'Huh? Yeah I did, it's just that I can sense something bad had happened here last night.'

'Something bad happens every few seconds in New York mate don't worry.'

We carried on walking up the lane between the buildings when I saw an elderly homeless man sat against the wall, shaking and looking as if he had been frightened by something.

'What do you think is wrong with him?' Blaze whispered.

'I think we should ask him, but I've got a bad feeling about this though.'

Blaze knelt down beside the man who didn't seem to notice we were here.

'Hey fella, are you ok?'

'Vampires,' he muttered, still staring blankly ahead.

'Vampires? Is that what he said?'

'Yeah, but look Jyrki, on his neck, two puncture holes. Oh my fucking god man,' Blaze jumped up from the floor.

'Oh fuck, I see. It wasn't me though, I've been at the apartment and so has Draven for the last day or two.'

'Then what the fuck is this? Jyrki, is he turning into a vamp?'

'No, the transformation won't take place unless he's almost drained. I'm more concerned with who done it at the moment.'

'Want me to call Draven?'

'Yes, tell him what we've just found and ask him what's the best thing to do. This poor guy looks like he's in deep shock; we'll need to bring him around quick. Go and get him some coffee whilst you're on the phone will you?'

'Sure, I'll be back in a minute.'

'Come on dude; come back to the real world,' I said, gently slapping his face.

The guy lifted his head up and looked at me.

'He bit me, a vampire, but there's no such thing as monsters,' he mumbled.

'Listen, I know you can hear me, ok. You're going to be alright, just hang in there. Can you remember what this...thing looked like that attacked you?'

The man looked at me sorrowfully. I knew instantly he wasn't lying.

'He...he was tall, dark hair. A bit like you, but, oh I'm sorry I couldn't really see to be honest with you, it was too dark and it all happened so quickly.'

'That's okay. My friend has gone to get you something to eat. I think you should see a doctor though to check out that wound.'

The man shook his head.

'No, no they'll throw me in the nut house. I've been on the streets for thirty years and I've never known anything like this.'

'Jyrki, what the fuck has gone on?'

'Stride, this guy was bitten by a vampire.'

'What vampire? You?' He pointed at me.

'No, not me, use your head, we've been with you for the last couple of days. He said this happened last night.'

'Here's his coffee,' Blaze said

Stride knelt down beside him and looked at his neck.

'Listen mate, you best get that neck cleaned up before you get an infection or something. Can I take you to the doctors?'

'I've just told your friend, no! Absolutely not. I'm fine, I'm sure it wasn't a vampire, could've been an animal.'

'An animal? Well if you remember anymore, can you please contact me? I'll give you my address ok,' he said as he took a small black notepad from his jacket pocket. 'Oh look and here's ten dollars, go and get some food ok?'

'Ah thank you, very kind of you.'

'Jyrki, come on,' Stride said as he pulled me away.

'That's it? We can't just leave him there?' I said

'Jyrki, the guy is unsure himself of what he saw, let him believe it was an animal ok. We know different. Now to work out where in hell this has come from.'

'What does Draven think it is?'

'He has no idea either. He wondered if it could've been Jimmy, in wolf form, but seeing the wound on the guy's neck now, I am certain it's a vampire bite mark.'

'Do you think Jimmy is up to something?' Blaze asked

'I do indeed. This has his name written all over it.'

As we walked to the van at the bottom of the lane, I couldn't help but look back at the poor guy sat on the ground with his grey coat wrapped around his shoulders. He was mumbling incoherently to himself between taking sips of his coffee. I felt saddened by his unfortunate circumstances and wished he would've seeked help from somewhere. It was another hard lesson to learn from the human world. You can't help those who do not wish to be helped.

I pulled the door open on the van and sat in the back seat. Stride tapped me on the shoulder.

'Don't let it get to you so much. The important thing is they didn't change him. I know it's hard to deal with but that's life mate. What I'm worried about is, whoever did this haven't done it to anyone else, unless...they knew you would be around.'

'You mean, this has been like a warning?'

'Yeah,' he nodded.

'That just gives us more to worry about,' Blaze said.

'How do you mean?'

'Well, it's obvious isn't it? They're tracking you, but how?'

'It could've been an inside job.' Stride suggested.

'Which could only mean one person and I don't want to even consider that right now.'

Stride shrugged and gazed out of the window. 'Well, best to keep it in mind that's all.'

We drove back to Blaze's place through the backstreets. Stride was still reeling over being betrayed by Jimmy.

'I can't fucking believe it y'know, that he's a wolf. All this fucking time and I didn't clock onto anything. When we were in Helsinki looking for you, Jyrki, I didn't even bother to question him how he knew where to look for you.'

'It's okay. There's no point in beating yourself up over it, you weren't to know.' I tried reassuring him.

'I get what you're saying, but you've got to understand, I trusted him. I feel like a fucking fool and besides, what if I told him about Draven huh?'

'But you didn't, so chill and help me think of what we're gonna do about this vampire.'

'If it's even a vampire,' Blaze said.

'Yeah, that's a thought but you never know, hell Jyrki wasn't even aware of Draven, so who fucking knows what's out there,' Stride said.

'Draven?' I yelled as I opened the door of the flat.

'There you all are. Did you find out anymore?' he said, standing up from the chair.

'No, we're certain it's a vampire mark. Luckily, the guy wasn't completely drained. Who the hell could it be?'

'Did you come across anymore vampires on your travels? Either of you?' Stride asked

'No, but...' I said, sitting down on the sofa.

'But what lad, spit it out?'

'In Finland, before I saw you on the bike, I met an old gypsy woman in Helsinki who seemed too had known about our existence. She told me her grandmother had been murdered by an unknown beast on the islands many years ago. If it wasn't you Draven... I wonder if she was talking about this guy.'

'The same woman who spoke with Jimmy and led us to the islands, supposedly was looking for you Jyrki.'

'What's this?' Blaze asked.

'We're guessing the other vampire is most certainly working for Jimmy. We need to find this guy as soon as possible, before he causes more harm than good to this city.'

'There's also something else, I'm afraid. I checked over the text with April's notebooks. It seems like she was already onto something. In here, she has written, 'returning back to the birth place,' with a question mark.

'What? What does that mean?'

'Whom is it implying though?' Stride asked.

'I assume it means Jyrki as it also mentions the Ankh. I don't like to say this but she has also death scribbled out on here too.'

'Me? Where am I going? When?' I panicked.

'I'm not quite sure when, but the birthplace is Egypt, if it means our race.'

'Egypt? When will I have time to get to Egypt? All this fucking shit is supposed to end by Halloween, which is tomorrow.'

'Don't shoot the messenger Jyrki, I'm just as frustrated and pissed off as you are.'

'Death? But you guys can't be killed. I thought you were already dead, sort of…aren't you?' Blaze asked.

'We're not exactly dead but then again we're not really living either. Death could also have a different meaning, like a new beginning…couldn't it?' I said, as I looked towards Draven for reassurance.

'You are exactly right. I say we need to get April out of there and fast. If anyone can help us now it's that's girl.'

'And I have the gig, I've completely forgotten about that,' Blaze said.

'Gig?' Draven shrugged. 'What's a 'gig'?'

'It's a rock concert. It's supposed to be the gig that will make or break the band. If it doesn't happen then I can kiss goodbye to my apartment and my car and more than likely I'll be single for the rest of my fucking life!'

'If this Apocalypse does happen, you will be single for eternity mate,' Stride laughed.

'The gig will happen; I'll make sure of it. Now, Jimmy asked us to meet him, yeah, so why don't we? Perhaps we can kill him there and then and get this shit over with. I'm sure we can get more information from Randulphr. That is, if I knew how to get hold of him. Does anyone have any ideas? They seem to appear when I least expect it, sort of give me the chills,' I said.

'They give you the chills, have you looked in a mirror lately?' Blaze said.

'Er, that's a good question, didn't anyone think of asking?' Stride said.

'They must be aware of what's going on? Maybe they'll be back later?' Blaze said with a cigarette hanging from his mouth.

'Yeah, I hope so. I'd like to know if they knew anything about the prophecy. There's so much I need to know.'

'So, we're going to meet this guy, a wolf?' Blaze said. 'And he isn't on our side? I don't like the sound of this.'

CHAPTER TWENTY-FOUR

I was feeling rather restless and fed up of hanging around the apartment all the time. It wouldn't have been so bad if it wasn't for Blaze interviewing me at every turn. I could appreciate he was fascinated by the revelation of vampires being real, but it was becoming borderline ridiculous. I mean, he even asked if I knew the real Count Dracula one night whilst we were watching some late night horror movies. I hadn't, but I knew of him. I suppose if I had, it would've been a highly amusing conversation. I guess by now we were all feeling a little tense and nervous, more so, Blaze than any of us. Draven and myself had to contend with the fact there was something unimaginable going to take place and soon. We had no solid evidence of who, what, why or when. Just some words written on an Ancient scroll we couldn't really decipher.

The door opened and in walked Stride clutching a plastic bag.

'Where have you been?' Blaze asked.

'Back to my place to get their lunch. Here Blaze, put this in the fridge will ya?'

'What is it?'

'What do you mean 'what is it?' It's blood, what else do you think they drink?'

Blaze took the bag, much to his dismay and walked into the kitchen.

'Don't make faces like that lad, it's better than having them bite you,' he laughed.

Stride sat down on the sofa then proceeded to pull his glasses from the inside of his jacket pocket.

'Right lads, let's all come up with a plan on getting April back safe and sound eh?' he said, sounding a little drunk.

'Stride, you do know there's much more to than this than saving April don't you? I said as I got up from the window sill.

'Of course, but first things first alright. I know you're worried.'

'Worried? I feel like I'm going out of my mind here,' I said, pacing around.

'Just calm yourself down, go and have a drink ok. Oi Blaze! Get that laptop thingy and find us a map of the area.'

It wasn't that I didn't care for April; I knew instinctively they wouldn't hurt her. My mind was so preoccupied with finding out where I was supposed to go and for whatever reason. I didn't know anything, and that was the worrying part. I couldn't even pick up anything intuitively. Draven and Blaze sat down beside me and under the dimly lit reading lamp we conceived a plan of action.

'Get us a map and some pictures of the hotel,' Stride ordered.

'According to the information, the penthouse where Jimmy is staying is five floors above ground,' Blaze said.

I was about to suggest climbing up the outside wall as I knew I had the strength to do so. Which was only when I was fully shifted.

'How about I take them by surprise? I'll climb up the wall?'

'Fucking hell, you're Spiderman now are ya?' Stride scoffed.

'You're fucking kidding; there are innocent people at the hotel,' Blaze blurted out.

Draven jumped to my defence.

'I am certain Jyrki can control it now Stride and it isn't half a bad idea. It will take them unawares if he's changed, plus it will give us ample opportunity to grab April and the scroll and get out of there.'

Stride tutted and mumbled something under his breath, I think it went something along the lines of 'I don't know why I bother.'

'Well, what's the next thing,' Blaze asked. 'Y'know, what Draven found out from the scroll...that there's something going on with the prophecy...?'

'We're not sure about that yet, here's hoping it will be mentioned in the missing piece and we find it before anything does happen.'

'You mean like an apocalypse...or something?' Blaze asked worriedly.

Draven and I looked at one another. I think our expression said it all. It was going on for 2am. We decided that we would take Draven's van and park it further up the street from the hotel, incase Jimmy had anyone on watch. The atmosphere was tense but with an air of excitement. I guess it was the adrenaline rush, but I was sure to have an even bigger rush in the next few moments.

'Don't worry Stride, I can control it,' I tried to assure him. Although I wasn't as hopeful as Draven.

'Right, okay when you're ready then,' he said unconvincingly and walked away.

'Thanks for the vote of confidence.' I didn't waste any time in saying. Blaze kept a lookout on the hotel security from the van. We were waiting until the security was due to change shifts. Once he had given us the signal, Draven and Stride would make their way to the hotel to get in.

The rain was beating down, which was no surprise. I pulled the hood of my hoody over my head and Stride tossed me a pocket knife.

'You're sure about this?' Blaze asked.

I was certain.

'Don't worry, I have it under control. No-one will see me.'

'Ok, best of luck then.'

Blaze couldn't bear to turn around and look at me. He stood with his hands in his pockets and kept a firmly fixed glare on the hotel doors. I knew it bothered him, but there was not much I could do right now.

Draven and Stride walked to the hotel whilst I stood waiting for the signal from Blaze. It did make me wonder why they would choose such a public place to meet, perhaps they didn't expect me to arrive in vampire mode. I really hope so. I stood motionless behind the van and sucked in some of the damp air. The street was quite deserted apart from an odd taxi passing by.

'Right, let's do this,' I said to myself, rolling up my sleeve. My hand began shaking again as I placed the knife over my forearm. As the blade touched my flesh, I paused. For some reason I had to check for the Ankh.

'Oh my fucking God! The Ankh has gone.' I dropped the knife on the floor and stood against the van unable to move. 'I had it at the flat,' I fretted; perhaps it had fallen off in the van. Nah, It's not supposed to leave me. Draven had heard me yelling and came running back up the street with Stride.

'It's gone!'

'What has?' Draven said looking concerned.

'The Ankh, here, look,' I said as I pulled down my t.shirt.

Draven shook his head in disbelief. 'It's not possible; sure you can't have dropped it?'

'Seriously, the thing hasn't left me in years, why now, when we have this to face?'

'Fuck knows, but we got to get in there, man, I don't know what else to fucking do.'

I was in pieces. An Ancient relic cannot just disappear, not one of this caliber.

Stride wiped his forehead of the sweat. 'We know that thing has powers beyond our comprehension, let's just go with that right now and hope for the best and we'll deal with this later, after we get April.'

Reluctantly I agreed, although the idea of shifting only a few hours before dawn wasn't my idea of a good night out. I took the pocket knife and rolled up my sleeve again. I hated to do this but it was the only way. The blood I had earlier was still in my system, so I had to entice the demon out somehow. It was the safest way. Even though it was frowned upon.

I craned my neck slightly to the left and caught sight of Blaze pacing up and down the pavement. I just had to go for it, cut my arm and hope for the best...well, after a small countdown. I screwed my face up and kept my eyes closed as I reached the number three in my head, then trying not to focus too much on the what if's I promptly made a small incision on my arm. Almost in an instant, it felt as though I had shut myself off in my head. The small jolt at the base of spine made me screech in agony as the demon squirmed around in joy. My face was next. I felt the rise in pain as the fangs cut through the gum. I gripped onto the mirror of the van and regrettably, I saw the transformation from my own eyes that were so very far away from the reality of now. I was now a monster. A disgusting leech that preyed on the innocent. Amongst the demonic chatter that plagued my brain, I managed to regain some of myself back. I had to focus on the task ahead and not fall prey to its demands.

Blaze whimpered and backed away from me. 'You don't have to fear me,' I said to him, covering half my face with the hood. 'You must trust me now, we have to work together. Just see past this face...please?'

'I'll try, er; I think you'd better go check out those two, looks like there's a problem,' he said as he pointed towards the hotel doors.

I walked a few yards down to the hotel and peered through the glass doors. I could see Draven and Stride having an argument with the woman on the reception desk.

'Oh no,' I couldn't just walk in there and cause alarm.

'Do you have a reservation?' She kept asking. I heard Stride mumble something in Gaelic and then promptly slammed his fist down on the desk. Draven tried to calm the situation down and I heard him ask for a room.

'Well, if it gets the job done,' he whispered to Stride.

'Blaze, go and park the van by the hotel doors and keep the back of the van open for us,' I whispered

'Sure, just get April out of there safe, please.'

'You can count on me, ok.'

I waited by the window until I saw them walk into the elevator. It was now time to finally sort this shit out once and for all. I sprinted towards the edge of building and began climbing, gripping virtually onto the wall with my fingernails. We were now running late and Jimmy was expecting Stride at any moment.

CHAPTER TWENTY-FIVE

'One. Two. Three!'

I shielded my eyes and kicked the balcony doors through with my foot. Shards of glass flickered through the air, falling and then embedding themselves into my flesh. I noticed Jimmy stood up from the leather chaise lounge at my surprise entrance, but only then to see I arrived with a friend of mine, which soon wiped the smug look from his face. I heard a click of a colt 45 to my left and with a swift arm movement; I hit the gun out of the guy's hand. He stumbled over the back of the chair and smacked his head on the minibar.

'Wasn't expecting this were you, huh?' I said, pointing to my face. 'Well, I guess you weren't expecting him too,' I said, pointing towards Draven who had just came through the door with Stride. Jimmy held his hands up as if he was about to give in when I saw the silver door handle turn on the adjoining room door. 'Is that April?' I asked. 'Is she ok?'

Something I was not expecting happened. Jimmy's smug look drew across his face again. I flicked a look at Stride, then Draven, who both then slowly turned their heads towards the door. I braced myself for the inevitable, when a young boy of about nineteen walked through. I heard Draven gasp as if he knew him. I started to panic, as my senses couldn't pick up whether he was human or not. Something was wrong, I was sure of it. He walked over to us confidently and I saw amongst that jet-black hair and small, startling grey eyes that looked at you wise beyond their years, my father. That was it, he reminded me of my father when he was young. But why, I wondered. Unless…

'Who the hell are you lad? I half expected Stride to be the first to question him. 'Is this your idea of a joke? You are going to set a teenager on us, well, well, where's your wolf pride Jimmy? Left it up your arse the last time you sniffed it?'

'Don't talk to me about pride when you, a stupid old fool trusted me with your precious information.'

'You may think that, but at least I wasn't a big enough fool to tell you about Draven,' Stride sniggered.

I noticed the boy kept glancing over towards Draven quite nervously.

Jimmy stood next to the boy with his arms folded looking so pleased with himself in his designer grey suit.

'This is Ryder.'

'Ryder? Who the fuck is Ryder? I fumed. 'Where is April? You asked us here, now where is she?' I think I yelled so loud the people on the next floor must've heard me.

Draven raised a hand as if to hush me up. He was still looking at the boy inquisitively.

'Why do I feel like I know you?' he said.

Stride walked over to me and nudged my arm. His face looked as pale as mine did. 'You know who he is don't you?'

I looked at him and shook my head. I had an idea though.

Stride raised his eyebrows and sighed.

'Yes, Draven, this is your son, but don't be fooled, he is already working for us,' Jimmy said.

Was this even possible? My head felt like it was about to explode with the madness here.

'Draven, please don't listen to him, he's bluffing. Let's get April and get out of here!'

'Oh you think so do you? Ryder say hello to your dad!'

I never knew Stride to stay quiet long enough.

'So is this part of your plan?' I demanded. 'You wanted us here, for what? The Ankh? So that thing there,' I pointed towards Ryder, 'can walk and terrorize this city in daylight, like how he attacked that homeless guy?'

Ryder remained quiet. He didn't look too aggressive; instead, there was a deeper sadness dwelling in those eyes of his as he looked at Draven.

'Where's the prophecy and April, did she decipher it for you?'

'April is in the adjoining room, and yes she has told us everything.'

'Well?' Although, I wasn't sure if I believed him. 'What did it say?'

'Let's say the Ancient God's should never have allowed Mardok to write his prophecies,' he sniggered. 'Because the only way you're going be free is when I put this stake through you. And I will stop you from returning the Ankh Jyrki, believe me and when I do there will be a rise of new bloods replacing every last mortal here on this earth...' he laughed. 'Just as it should've been before these humans evolved.'

'And what are you gaining from all of this?'

'I will be gaining what is so rightfully mine, what I have been seeking for since Mardok threw me out of the Temple. I shall have that Ankh and the power of the Ancient Gods will be mine. YOU and the rest of this pathetic world will be worshipping me.'

'Well, you're gonna have a hard time without the Ankh,' I laughed. 'Because, I don't have it.'

I realised it wasn't such a laughing matter at all. On the wall behind Jimmy, I saw the reflection of the sun from the window as it was coming up over the horizon. 'Oh shit!' I whispered.

Draven must've been on the same wavelength as me as I saw him walk behind Jafar discreetly and push him onto the floor.

Feeling this was an opportune moment to get out I yelled to Stride to get April from the other room.

Things began to turn chaotic. Ryder, who was not so quiet anymore leapt towards me. I was shocked by the power he had for a half vampire. He hissed and glared into my face as he held me down onto the floor. I heard two shots coming from the back of the chair, headed towards the door where April was.

'Draven – get April, please.' I screamed. The sound of the shot resonated in my brain. I willfully tried to push Ryder off me but his strength was that of steel. I had not encountered anything like him. With all the strength I could muster, the thought of April and Stride hurt or worse suddenly brought out the worst in me I had ever known. I gripped Ryder around the neck and threw him against the wardrobe. I rolled over on the floor before getting up onto my feet to see Draven tackle the guy I had hit earlier with the gun. Another shot was fired and the alarms eventually went off. Jimmy was out cold on the floor and the last thing I was expecting to see when I swerved my head around, was Ryder who had already come up behind me, and began pushing me towards the window. This was all I could remember as I felt the warmth of the sun on my skin as I heard Blaze's screams from down below...

CHAPTER TWENTY-SIX

I could feel so much heat, much more than I've ever been used to. My whole body was in a state of relaxation. As my thoughts connected with my senses I realised I was laying down on a concrete floor with my eyes shut. I shot up from the floor and gasped. For some strange reason my whole body was covered in sweat. Am I dead now. Is this how it's supposed to be. I placed a sweaty palm on my bare chest and felt a slight pulsating movement. 'No, this can't be?' I feared. I took a deep breath, trying to remain calm, when I glanced around and saw the room I was in wasn't somewhere I recognised. It was bare and hollow and only lit by a few torches on the wall. What was I doing here? I certainly felt different too. There was no possible way I could be human, could there.

'Oh fuck,' I whispered.

I could hear the sound of footsteps approaching me. They seemed not far in the distance either, but every step seemed to had taken age to shift to the next. One step followed by the resonated echo of the other. I stared into the blackness and waited with instilled terror at what it would uncover. All my vampire senses were gone and I have never been more vulnerable. Suddenly, the sound halted, and I could feel the pounding of my heart beating against my chest. I sat waiting in anticipation of what I would find.

Slowly, an arm, that looked very much human lifted the torch from the wall and pulled it close to their chest. I kept my eye on the flicker of the golden flame as it walked towards me. The anticipation was gnawing away at me and I couldn't bring myself to say anything. Then, finally, the voice belonging to the body it inhabited, spoke.

'Jyrki, I bid you welcome.'

The voice was calm and unthreatening. My guess was it belonged to an old man, of some sort. Was he human though, that was my concern.

I hesitated to say anything. He held the torch in front of my face and I could hear him mutter to himself.

'Yes, you are Amroath's son alright.'

Father, he knows Father.

The shock of hearing my father's name was far too much to

comprehend especially in my human like state. I took a step back from the intense heat of the flame and stumbled backwards onto the hardness of the concrete floor.

'I am Mardok, keeper of the Secret Order; I have been waiting for you for many years...'

Now I had a face to the name. The man must've been at least five foot, with silver hair. He had a friendly face, but looked tired, as if he had lived through endless time. He had one hand clutching onto a walking stick and was wearing a brown robe.

'Where am I?'

'We have much to discuss, please, come...'

He gestured me to follow him, which I did. I walked about ten yards when he stopped by a secured door. Mardok just waved his hands over the locks and they unbolted by themselves. I looked on in amazement. Not even I had this kind of gift. Just as I was about to ask who he was really, the outside of his world was revealed to me.

No wonder I was hot. The dry Egyptian heat began to play havoc with my chest. I coughed and spluttered as we stepped outside the door. If that wasn't all, the intense glare of the sun pained my eyes so bad; I had to cover them with my arm. Then it hit me. I was standing in the sunlight for the first time without the Ankh.

Mardok continued to walk ahead, with one hand grappling onto his wooden walking stick and the other waving about in mid-air for me to follow him. I turned back and saw I had come from the Temple of Osiris.

'You will experience new things here, just take them for what they are. It is only temporary.'

'Temporary? Am I human?'

'For now. The beast has no business here.'

I lowered my arm and allowed my eyes to adjust to the light before walking any further, but the intensity of the light reflecting off the sand made it so hard to focus. The golden pyramid standing so magnificently in front me, made me feel as if I was nothing at all. I was seeing things with my eyes for the first time as a human.

My legs ached and I was thirsty. Mardok somehow knew what I was thinking.

'You will get refreshments in a moment, please step inside here.' He pushed the stele at the west side of the pyramid, which I could only fathom that it was not visible to the naked eye. I looked around at the vast desert before entering; it was eerily quiet and deserted of life.

'So what is this place?' I asked, as I entered the building. In front of me was a long narrow passage, which became darker the more you descended down. Part of me was having second thoughts about all this when Mardok pointed towards a small room to my right. As I walked in, the room instantly lit with many white candles. I panned my vision around the burnt ochre walls that were full of scrolls stacked on wooden shelving and many Egyptian artifacts placed neatly on a wooden chest.

'Come and sit down,' he pulled out a carved wooden chair for me, then one for himself. I watched him as he struggled to pour some red wine into a goblet.

'Here, let me help.' His hands were shaking and he smiled and apologised.

'You have to forgive me; I am not as young as I was.'

'So, you're Mardok? Who are you really and what am I doing here?'

'Jyrki, have you ever wondered why in life some questions are better left unanswered? Because if we knew it all, what would we strive to live for, hm? I have been here since time began, some may argue I am time, but that is irrelevant right now.'

'What do you mean by time?'

'When the Ancient Gods ruled Egypt, they had in their possession many gifts, magic, power, wealth beyond your imagination, but what they didn't have under all that knowledge was the wisdom to see into the future, to see the destruction it would play out for mankind, the simplest of beings.'

'I take it you're not human then...vampire?'

'Me? Oh no, I was one of the Gods aides that held that power until I came to possess a new sight, I was here when your kind was created by Ramesses and despite my poorly efforts to stop it from happening, I entrusted your father to take the Ankh as far away from Egypt as he could.'

'Hang on, you're an Ancient prophet, but you can't do anything to stop Ryder and the Others? I mean, I still don't know who they are or whose side they are on.'

Mardok wove his hand in the air and shook his head.

'Wait! You have to forgive me, the others work for me...and they are not your enemy, even though it seems that way. The one who killed your family was Ryder...and to your second question, no I cannot. I am nothing more than an old man now, besides I am not able to dabble in the future, just here to oversee things.'

'So how the hell have you survived?'

'I am an immortal, just like you. I have to ensure the human race will not be subjected to the unnatural order of things...things my peers created. I've lived in that temple for so long, waiting for this moment I saw a very long time ago.'

'So, the Others, what are they?'

'Yes I wondered if you would be curious enough to ask about them.' He paused for a moment and called out for Randulphr, but he didn't come.

'Hm, these wolves can be very fickle creatures...'

'I know him,' I muttered. 'And the Ankh? Where is it?'

'You have many questions, but first thing, the prophecy, the future I foresaw, is happening now. You must kill Ryder with the Serpents Sword; it is the only way to stop Jimmy getting hold of the Ankh. However, Jyrki, this is the important thing, you must do this before midnight, Halloween otherwise the dead will be walking the earth, and everything the world had come to know, will be wiped. The Ankh has served you well until now, but when you go back, you must do what I have asked.'

'But, he's Draven's son...is there any other way?'

'There is always another way Jyrki, but in order for that to happen Jafar must be stopped to save Ryder. You will face these hounds and you must kill every one of them before they end up causing too much damage. Jimmy is Jafar. You do know that don't you?'

'You're telling me, Jimmy is Jafar... a wolf?'

'He isn't who or what you think he is. Your good friend Stride has been duped into believing Jimmy could help him with the prophecy. Jimmy use to work for me within the Secret Order, but he soon was caught up in the greed and power. He has searched for you for years and when he stole the prophecy and found out about Ryder, well, they have been working together since. He is known here as the bringer of the Apocalypse.'

'So that's why the Ankh couldn't be returned?'

'Yes, because you would've become mortal before you have completed your destiny. Jyrki, we never chose you, your father did. He saw within you great potential. Draven has his own destiny to fulfill. Now, you must return, back to New York. The Ankh shall be with you, but remember, midnight Halloween. The curse will lift only once it's done, and please...try and not read the rest of the prophecy before. It is integral you don't.'

'Really? But I don't have it.'

'Yes, some things are best left as they are. I had only written the first prophecy when I was fortunate or rather unfortunate enough to witness the end. I was instructed not to do so but I wrote it for my own selfish reasons. Don't worry though, you are being protected.'

'By whom? Those things I saw in the woods?'

He looked as if he didn't want to say much more.

'Er, yes. Have you heard of Anubis? Protector of the dead? When you see him, he will offer you great advice. But these Gods don't show themselves freely. He is part of my Secret Order, to ensure Jafar and his protégés don't cause too much damage on Earth. We know them as the Hounds of The Apocalypse. They will bring horrendous change to mankind if you don't stop them.'

'Anubis?'

'Yes, Anubis is what he represents, his name is Randulphr. So now it's time for you to go back.'

'Randulphr? I've already met him.'

'Yes, and he is keeping you informed. Have patience and he will come to you.'

He struggled to get off the chair and gestured me with his thin, boney hand to walk back out of the Pyramid. I couldn't possibly leave without asking the one thing which bothered me since I arrived here. I stood up from my seat and hesitated for a moment.

'You want to know why you are human?' he said, beating me to it.

'Yes...'

'Because Jyrki,' he gestured around with his arm, 'this place is the thin veil between your world and the next. Here you represent who you truly are.'

'Who I truly am? What's that?'

'You'll know when the time comes.'

He walked me to the wooden door. As he opened it, he paused.

'I won't come any further, you know the way back.'

I stood in the desert with the most uncomfortable feeling of the sand between my toes. I looked over to the small stone building I came from and then back to Mardok.

'My father, he mentioned you once.'

'Amroath was a good man just as you are. I couldn't have chosen two better people to take care of the Ankh.'

With that, he bowed his head and closed the door.

CHAPTER TWENTY-SEVEN

'Jyrki!'

I heard my name being called. Just as I was about to wake up, I felt a stinging sensation across my left cheek.

'Jyrki! Wake up man.'

My eyes flickered open to see Blaze leaning over me slapping me across the face.

'Blaze, what the fuck are you doing?'

'You've got to get up, Stride has got April out and they're waiting in the van, quick, before the cops turn up.'

Blaze held out his hand and pulled me up from the floor. I was feeling slightly dizzy and almost keeled over. He reached out to catch me from hitting the pavement again when I noticed he was still looking at me with wide eyes.

'Hang on...I need to check something first,' I felt my chest and the Ankh, sure enough was there.

I was aware I was receiving strange looks off the public who more than likely had seen me fall a hundred feet out of the window then get up as if nothing had happened. I glanced around at the small crowd that had gathered by the entrance of the hotel steps and shrugged, 'I was, um...practicing a stunt.'

'Come on...'

Blaze yelled at me and began frantically pointing to the back doors. As I ran towards the back of the van it became apparent to me that April was holding the doors open for me.

'What happened to you? I was told you didn't have the Ankh,' she shouted.

'April?' I threw my arms around her petite frame and held her tightly against my body. I was in love with her but couldn't say it. I only hoped she felt the same way.

'What happened to you? I thought you were a goner,' Stride yelled from the front seat.

'How long did I disappear for?' I asked

'Disappear?'

'Yes, I did didn't I?'

Blaze looked at me through the rear view mirror and shook his head.

'Jeez, Jyrki you gave me a fucking scare man, when I saw you fall from that window, I thought you would've turned to dust or something. You didn't have the Ankh when you went in there did you. So what the hell happened?'

'You mean to say I didn't go anywhere? I just landed on the pavement?'

'Yeah! Why, what happened?'

'I went to Egypt.'

'What? What the fuck are you talking about?' Stride shrieked

'That could've been possible,' April quipped, as she almost slipped off the seat.

I reached out to catch her from falling.

'How do you mean it's possible?'

'Well, from what I read the Ankh is supposed to hold mysterious energy, so I wouldn't be surprised if what you're saying is actually true.'

I suddenly noticed Blaze had put his foot down on the gas and we were almost speeding down Times Square.

'Blaze, why the fuck are we speeding?'

'Oh you didn't notice that lot trailing behind us?'

I looked out of the window and saw Jimmy's people chasing us in black cars.

'Where's Draven?'

'We don't know. He was holding Ryder off of chasing us as we left the building,' April said.

I didn't know what to think, or do. 'Blaze, when is Halloween?'

'Tomorrow and we have that gig, I may aswell cancel the fucking thing now.'

'No, don't do that. There has to be another way.'

As we got onto the Brooklyn Bridge, bullets were now pounding the van. I shielded April the best I could as Blaze kept a steady hand on the steering wheel.

'Fucckkk! My fucking van, I hope the government is going to compensate me for saving the fucking world,' he raged.

Stride took his rifle from the dashboard and wound down the window. 'Take this ya fucking bastards!' he yelled.

April rested her head onto my chest. I felt her body quiver with fright. 'It's going to be okay.' I whispered.

'Where are we going? The police will be all over us and… and Ryder will find us...' she sobbed.

'Shhh! You're safe with me.'

I saw Blaze at the corner of my eye, watching me from the mirror. He must've caught onto my gaze and gave me an assuring wink.

Stride unbuckled his seatbelt and opened the van door. We were still going about eighty miles an hour and heading towards the end of the bridge.

'I'll fucking stop 'em!' he yelled.

He held onto the back of his seat and with the other hand fired a few shots at the car that was unnervingly close. The other motorists swerved away at the sight of Stride and the gun.

'Got his fucking wheels.'

'So, now where are we headed to?' I asked.

'We'll go to my mate's recording studio in Manhattan, he's away right now,' Blaze said. 'It's the only place I can think of.'

Blaze slammed his foot on the break

'We're here! He hasn't exactly finished the inside yet, but, what the fuck am I on about...who cares.'

'No cops?' Stride asked before he would open the door.

I looked out of the back window of the van.

'No, we've lost them.'

'I'll park it out of sight then, here's the key, I'll see you in a minute.'

I lifted April off the floor and helped her out of the van. She still looked shaken up from her ordeal. Her hair, which had always been pulled back into a ponytail was now down and draped over her shoulders. For the first time in a while, I noticed she didn't have her glasses on and I was able to see her beautiful heart shaped face. I ran my eyes over her delicate, feminine features. Her stunning green eyes and her small, slightly turned up nose made me smile; as I did, I noticed her cheeks began to glow. I wondered to myself what it would be like to live as a human and do normal human things, like have relationships. Then I snapped out of my daydream to sound of Stride calling me into the studio.

'C'mon, c'mon, get in here before anyone sees ya.'

'I'll be there in a second. April…' I called as she began walking through the door.

'What is it?' she said, still sounding a little pissed off from her ordeal.

'I, er just wanted to say...' Then I was rudely interrupted by Blaze, again.

'You can't be standing around when you're on the run, get the fuck in there!'

Blaze ushered me through the door. He gripped my arm and pulled me back into the small reception area.

'Listen, I don't think she knows you're a...well, you know that you're different. I'm not completely stupid, I know you have feelings for her, but now isn't the right time.'

I couldn't very well argue with him, he knew April best and all I wanted was for her to be happy. I gave Blaze a friendly pat on the shoulder and nodded. He could see that I was in love with his sister.

'Hey,' he smiled. 'You'd make a great couple though; just get this business sorted out first ok.'

I was happy to oblige.

CHAPTER TWENTY-EIGHT

'Here, take this and drink it in there, I don't want April seeing anything...' Blaze whispered, handing me sachet of blood.

'You're getting brave aren't you?' I laughed.

'Well, what's the point in living in denial? I have a vampire for a friend; I suppose they don't come any cooler than that.'
I smiled and gratefully took the sachet out of his hand.

'There's a toilet just down the hallway, get it down you because I don't want you changing. It freaks me out if truth be known.'

'Thanks, and er, thanks for being so understanding...'

'Yeah, yeah yeah, it's cool mate. I'd better go and see what Stride is up to, hope he's not fucking about with the equipment. The guy is completely off it...did you see how he stood firing out the door?'

'Yeah, I sometimes wonder if he's all there too.'

'So, we'll figure out what we're going to do in a bit. I guess we're all in this together now huh?'

'You have no idea how good it feels to hear that...seriously.'
We walked out of the reception area, through the long corridor. Blaze pointed out the toilets to the left and walked into the studio.

Bitterly, I threw the sachet of blood into the sink and looked at my reflection in the mirror. This was the first chance I had on which to reflect on what had happened in Egypt. I ran my hand down my long, chiseled face that was merely a shadow of my former self and stared long and hard into my ice blue eyes. Eyes, which seemed to be weighed down with all that I had seen in my life. The hunger was calling, but I was reeling with hate and anger towards it. I began to shake and the overwhelming feeling of despair washed over me. I crossed my arms over my chest for some self-comfort, but the next thing I knew my rage reached to a point where I just couldn't take it anymore.

'Damnit,' I yelled, throwing the sachet of blood at the mirror.
Not giving any thought to the consequences, I raised my fist and lunged it quite forcefully at the mirror. It was as if everything was now playing out in slow motion from this point on. I sank to the floor, weeping in bitter desperation for a miracle. My hand began to ache. Unfortunately

this was the human side of me showing. How intriguing that pain was my only connection to being mortal. I looked at my fist. It was completely gashed. I pulled out some of the protruding glass that embedded itself into my knuckles and flicked them to one side. I just did not want to drink the blood anymore.

'Jyrki!? Are you okay. Oh, fuck! What's happened?' Blaze said as he burst through the door.

I looked up at Blaze and Stride. Inside I was screaming for their help. My lips began to quiver as I felt the tingling sensation of the fangs breaking through the gum. 'I can't drink this shit anymore...I want to be normal. I want to be like you, to walk in the sun and never have to worry about turning to dust. I want someone to love me for me and not have people walk past me in the street with fear,' I said, shaking like an addict needing another fix.

Stride knelt down beside me and shook his head in a pitiful way. 'You best to drink it right now and then we can talk about what happened in Egypt ok? I'm sure Draven is out there safe and he wouldn't want to see you like this.'

'What's going on?'

'April get the hell outta here!'

Blaze tried to push April out of the door, but she was trying to fight her way back in.

'What's happened? Blaze let me through the fucking door alright,' she screamed.

I could tell by the way the colour had drained from Blaze's face that he was devastated, that she had seen me looking like this.

'I didn't want you to see him like this sis, I wanted to protect you.'

'Protect me?' She said still looking at me with wide eyes. 'Why would you need to protect me from him? I knew what he was right from the very first moment I met him.'

Blazes' face looked as if it was about to crack under pressure.

'What did you just say sis?'

I lifted my head up, feeling almost spun out by what I had just heard.

'Really? You've always known that I was a vampire?'

'Of course I have. The Ankh confirmed it for me. You see, I was the one who uncovered the prophecy...I knew about the Egyptians and the Vampires, but Dr. Matthews had sworn me not to say anything. It was

Jimmy who had killed him because he knew too much. I guess he didn't account for me in that until I went back to the office that afternoon.'

'Bloody hell...' Stride muttered. 'Sorry, no pun intended lad.'

'Jyrki?'

April's sweet voice calmed me like no other.

'Drink the blood before you shift, please. Then we can help you.'

She handed me the sachet and reluctantly I drank.

'I'm sorry for this...I don't know what came over me.'

I pulled my sleeve and wiped the excess blood from my mouth, feeling slightly embarrassed by it all.

'No harm done. Now tell us what happened earlier, when you fell from the window. Where did you go, tell us everything?' Stride said calmly.

'It was the oddest thing. All I remember is seeing Ryder push me out of the window and then waking up in a strange, dark and humid room. But I was different there, I wasn't a vampire. I was human, with a heartbeat. I can remember the heat being unbearable and feeling very insecure without my vampire strength.'

'You were human, really?' April said.

'Yes. Then I heard footsteps coming towards me. I wanted to get up from the floor but I just didn't have the strength. I felt fear, human fear and I didn't like it at all. I was expecting the worst, but out of the shadows came an old man, very old, short and clasping a walking stick. He said he knew Father and he was expecting me.'

'Carry on...' Stride was getting impatient.

'His name was Mardok. He told me he was an ancient prophet to the Egyptian Gods...'

'Was an Ancient prophet?' April asked interestedly.

I nodded.

'Yes, he was present at the birth of the vampires in Egypt. He was the one who gave my father the Ankh for safekeeping until the time came to return it.'

'And when does it need returning?' Blaze asked

'Mardok wrote the prophecy as he had foresight into the future, he saw Ryder and Jimmy, who I'm sorry to say this Stride, just happens to be Jafar, an Ancient member of the Secret Order, an understudy to Mardok.'

'You're fucking joking...' Stride gasped.

'The Ankh will be returned as soon as I get rid of Ryder, by Halloween.'

'That's less than 24 hours away...how are you going to manage that?' Blaze asked.

'I have an idea, but Ii don't know what good it'll do.'

CHAPTER TWENTY-NINE

There was something about my reflection staring back at me from the glass in the sound engineering room that just didn't look like me anymore. Maybe I had come to realise what I was seeing was an empty shell, a souless living creature that held no worth. Day to day I would consistently fight against who I really am and who I wanted to be, but the most difficult was fighting against what I didn't want the world to see; especially to those who mattered. Tonight, being the exception of course. My fears about April knowing what I am were realised but despite the shame, I was relieved about her reaction.

We didn't know how long we had until Jimmy would find us, so we needed to find out as much as we could while we had a chance. We really could've used Draven right now for more details on Ryder, as he was still a mystery to us, but there was nothing to do but wait and hope April would find something online. I could hear her tapping on the keys from the other room so I got up to join them in the reception area. I stood by the doorway and April's eyes met mine. She smiled and patted the seat of the brown leather couch for me to join her.

'I've gone over every file I have on the reign of Ramesses, but there's nothing, not even a mention of the vampires or the Blood War. Jyrki,' she said, peering over the black rim of her glasses, 'what about the last piece of the prophecy, the one Jimmy had me wanting to decipher?'

'No! That's another thing I forgot to mention. Mardok told me never to read it. Something to do with not knowing what's in your future - you didn't decipher it did you because Jimmy said you had?'

'No, I couldn't, it's written in a very peculiar ancient language, different to that of the first piece. I told him a load of bollocks to shut him up. I'm wondering if they were written in two different era's though.'

'Then I have no idea. I think we have exhausted every lead. But if only we had the book too...'

'Don't worry; the book is safe in my bag. I sneaked it under my top when Stride got me out of the hotel. And I did manage to get a look at it actually, it mentioned something about, er...let me think...the serpent sword should penetrate the demon flesh but then in order to break the curse one must take the book and recite the Spell of The Anubis. Does that make sense to you?' she shrugged.

'Well, that's what Mardok told me, but there's something I don't understand...why was Draven saved that day, maybe Ryder knew he was his father and let him go?'

Stride, who was dozing off on the chair leapt up.

'You mean to say Ryder killed the New Bloods?'

'Yes, and all along I thought it was the Others. You see, Father was expecting them that day as they are the ones with the authority on the ankh, but I remember Draven saying he could sense something darker... oh I just don't understand it...you don't think Ryder and Draven are in this together do you, I mean, do you see him here?'

'That's true, but he didn't know of Ryder's existence though did he?' April said, still engrossed in whatever she was reading on the computer.

'Have you ever thought he has been protecting him?' Stride asked 'Because, I remember that day I met him in that pub, he mentioned a lot of things that didn't quite add up.'

'Really? But like what exactly?'

Stride pulled his chair closer to me. A worried frown drew across his face and it looked as if he was reliving the moment in his head before he began to tell me.

'Even though I was drunk that night, some of the things he said seemed to had stuck with me, for whatever reason. Thinking back now, when I asked him about how he came to know about your whereabouts he mentioned Jim... then trailed off onto something else. I never gave it a thought at the time. Funny how things come back to you after all these years. Also he was adamant that he should be kept a secret to you...until the time was right. Maybe I'm making a big thing out of nothing, but I have a feeling he knew Jimmy long before I did. And, if he knew Jimmy then he'd know about Ryder...'

'So, the question is then are The Others on our side?' April asked 'Even that wolf?'

'That's what I'd like to know. Although Mardok did say Randulphr would give us information, so that confirms it for me. You know, my Father always said they were superior to us...so if they didn't kill my clan then it had to be Ryder, like Mardok says. But the question is how? One-half vampire to slain them all? It doesn't seem feasible.'

'The Others, you say works for Mardok? You don't suppose they knew about Draven siring a half vampire child, which led to them discovering your whereabouts? Maybe Jimmy had already been informed and got there first? Y'know, before Randulphr could get there to warn you.' April said, still tapping away at the laptop.

'Hm, yeah I wonder...I think I really should speak with Mardok again, but I have no idea how in the hell to reach him. We've only got less than 24 hours.'

'You did say you had a plan?' Blaze asked

'Yeah I do...'

Stride's mobile rang, cutting me off.

'Jyrki, the call is for you!' he said, handing me his mobile.

'Me?' Whom do I know?

'Hi?' I said.

'It's Draven, look I don't have much time, so meet me now at the Bat Cave...it's a bar, Blaze will know where it is. And please trust me, alright. I'm on your side.'

He hung up before I could say anything.

'Who was it?' Stride asked looking a little pale.

'It was Draven, he says he wants to meet me at the Bat Cave, he said Blaze will know where it is,' I shrugged.

Everyone stopped what they were doing and looked at me. I could see by their facial expressions that they felt it was a bad idea.

'He's my brother though, what possible harm could he do to me?'

Blaze shook his head and Stride rubbed his chin, mulling over all the worst-case scenarios that could arise.

'Are you sure about this? What if he isn't on our side and he has Ryder and Jimmy with him? Those three together could cause Armageddon just sitting down for a pint.'

'Yeah, good point. What good would two mortals and one vampire be against that lot?'

April didn't look too convinced either.

'Personally, it's up to you what you do, and whatever you decide we'll back you up, but didn't you say you had a plan?'

'I was thinking, as it's Halloween tomorrow and it's the gig, why don't we entice them there? Make it out to be part of the show, so that way nobody becomes suspicious.'

'Well, let's find out what Ryder is capable of first, we can't really let them mingle amongst the humans, that would be asking for trouble.'

'Yes, but think about it, we can't let the humans know what is going on either, it was part of the deal with the Ancient God's. I don't want to be responsible for altering world history. Or is there another way?'

'There must be. Let's wait until that wolf shows up again,' Stride said.

CHAPTER THIRTY

'Where is this club?' I asked Blaze.

'It's an underground club, not far from here.'

'You mean it's underground?'

'Yeah, but it has been boarded up for a few years now.'

'Why would he want to meet us there?' Stride muttered.

'Have you ever thought it's safer for him and its dark?' April said.

'C'mon then, let's go now, see what the hell is happening,' Stride said, stumping out his cigarette on the floor.

We had gone fifteen minutes up the road when Blaze began to slow the van down. Many of the properties had rental or for sale signs outside. It looked like the usual breeding ground for the addicts and the tramps to spend their time.

'Here it is,' Blaze said, pointing to a red brick building, 'I use to come to this place when I was a kid. I saw The Clash here once in the mid-eighties. I can't believe the state gone on it now.'

'Bloody hell, he must've done some walking last night to end up here,' Stride said.

'There's an entrance just there,' Blaze said pointing to a boarded up door, 'Jyrki, go and see if you can pull it open.'

We all got out of the van and walked towards the building. A few youngsters walked by and gave the usual scowl and look of disapproval. I had come to accept this as normal now and walked gracefully past them.

'Let me help you,' Stride said trying to pull the board off.

'It's fine,' I sniggered. 'I am more than capable. Er, April, maybe it's best if you wait in the van?'

'I'll wait outside the van, ok? Believe me you me, I am much tougher than I look.'

'I didn't mean it like that…' I said; feeling slightly pissed off that I had annoyed her.

April smiled. 'I was kidding, but I will wait here alright. Don't worry about me too much.'

'Ok, just be careful alright,' I said to her, nodding towards the youngsters watching us.

'I see, ok! Now go.'

I walked down the steep, narrow staircase into blackened room. A single candlelight flickered and shone on top of the bar.

'Draven, are you here?'

'This is a fucking trap, I know it,' Stride said, ever the pessimist.

I raised my hand to hush him up.

'I'm here, but I'm not too good. Ask Stride to get us some blood and keep the humans away Jyrki. I can't deal with smelling their blood right now.'

'He's behind the bar. Stride, quick, get the blood from the van.'

'I'm on it.'

My eyes were used to the dark; in fact, I used to think I saw better at night than day. My instinct was also highly tuned in the darkness and as soon as I reached the last step, I knew our assumptions about him were wrong.

I crouched down beside him. He was shaking and in full vampire. Miraculously he had managed to chain himself to the bar before he could do any serious damage.

'I'm here, what the fuck happened?'

'I couldn't risk going back to Stride's place for food. I was lucky enough to escape Jafar.'

'How did you contact us?'

'Stride dropped his phone at the hotel. I was so hungry and afraid of killing someone Jyrki.'

'It's okay now. So, um…is Ryder really your son?'

'Yes,' he nodded.

'Here's the blood. Jyrki you best give it to him,' Stride said

'Here, take this. So you only found out about Ryder this morning?'

'Yes, I didn't even know about him, I swear. He's my son, my son.'

'Stride reckons you knew about Jimmy long before he did, is this true?'

Draven struggled to sit up. I undid the chain and helped him up from the floor.

'Listen Jyrki, there is something I didn't tell you.'

I didn't like this sound of this.

'I, er, may have left some details out when I spoke about the last day at the compound. Before I was knocked unconscious, I saw Jimmy in his wolf form…'

'You what?'

'Yes, we were all in hiding when they came. I was stood behind the tree at the edge of the compound when I saw father walk towards this wolf. I assumed he was trying to strike a deal with him but by the expression on fathers face, I don't think this wolf was what he was expecting. I heard him telepathically say his name was Jafar and all hell broke loose, the next thing I know I'm out cold.'

'So father was expecting Randulphr then? The Others didn't want to kill us.'

'That's the way it looks right now.'

'Draven, did you vamps know you could have kids?' Blaze asked

'Of course, but it was forbidden to even enter a relationship with a woman, especially a human one. It was part of the agreement we had. But I'd love to know what happened to his mother,' he wept

'Where's Ryder now? Why is he working for them?'

'He was abandoned by his mother when he was five. As soon as he started biting her and craving blood, her family, who were superstitious anyway decided to abandon him in the woods. It must've been when the ancients caught on. But it seems like Jimmy had got there first.'

'Fuck! Vampire babies, now that's an even scarier thought,' Blaze said

'So what did they want with him?'

'They wanted him to get to us for the Ankh. That's why the Others were sent to protect us that day because they knew what was going to happen. If they get their hands on the Ankh, jimmy will spill our blood, but worse than that, he'll open the gates to underworld and change the entire human race into monsters. Imagine how catastrophic that would be?'

'But why?'

'Because he was betrayed by Ramesses.'

'What? Is that you Randulphr, where are you?'

Randulphr walked out of the shadow into the glimmer of the candlelight.

'When the Blood War broke out, Ramesses had already ordered Amroath with the serpents' sword. He trusted Mardok to give it to him to protect, as he feared it would end up in the wrong hands. Once all the vampires were killed, Jafar, who was once nothing more than a guardian of the temple, like us, sought revenge on Amroath in order to take the sword, until he realised the Ankh would enable him to walk in daylight. He also knew something about the sword we did not know at the time. It is the only weapon to kill immortals.'

'The sword father gave you?' I said to Draven.

'Do you still have it?'

'Of course, it's safe at Blaze's place.'

'So the sword has something to do with the ending of the prophecy? But what?'

'As you know, the future is not really ours to speak of. We are only here to ensure you do your part.' Randulphr explained.

'But what about Mardok? Why was I sent back, is there anyway of me going back again?'

'You entered into another realm; it wasn't Egypt as it is today. The Ankh had saved you from falling out into the sunlight because you are part of something bigger than all of us. I am not entirely sure if you could go back again.'

'I am aware there is going to be a fight for this Ankh. Jimmy mentioned something about central Park, tonight?'

'It all has to end tonight; it was the way it was written. Do you have the prophecy and the Book?' Randulphr asked.

'Yes, but we can't decipher the last text on the prophecy. Should we know what it says?'

'No, you mustn't. The spell is the only thing you're going to need and I trust April can decipher this for you?'

'Yes, I'm sure she can.' Stride said.

'Was April a part in this, the prophecy I mean?' I asked.

'You all were. The world is a very mysterious place. It's far too complex for a human mind to understand. Anyway, I have to go, but we'll be back when you need us.'

'Hang on, before you go. How does Jimmy shift into a wolf? Is there anything we should know about?'

'Yes, there is something. He cannot shift into wolf form in daylight; after all, he is one of the creatures of the darkness himself. Just don't underestimate him. Wolves can be very cunning and manipulative, which is the reason why we were chosen to protect the secrets.'

'Is there a blanket in the back of the van?' Blaze asked

'What for?' Stride said

'To cover Draven.'

'It's ok, I have one here I took from the hotel.'

'Right, c'mon let's get out of this place, it's giving me the creeps,' Blaze said.

'And I need something to eat too,' I said.

CHAPTER THIRTY-ONE

It all ends tonight. Whether the prophecy is in my favour or not I do not know. My fate is now placed in the hands of the Ancient God's. As if that thought didn't sit like a dark depression on my shoulders, these people, whom I've come to regard as my dearest friends, would find themselves living their lives as I have done for the last hundred and nineteen years. Jafar's dealings with the underworld would cost this world so much more than immortality. That was something I could not let happen. As long as I had the faith of my father within me, I was prepared to put my life on the line for the human race, as after all it looks like this was written long before I ever came into this world.

'Jyrki, you're gonna be alright,' April said, as if she was reading my thoughts.

I tried to force a smile just to reassure her, but I couldn't. I took a hold of her hand and placed a sincere, delicate kiss on the back. This wasn't something I normally did, so I felt quite surprised by my actions. Realising what I had done, I turned to look away, slightly embarrassed incase Draven had seen me. April didn't say anything but the feeling of her shoulder against mine said a lot more than words ever could.

The van was silent, which was doing nothing for my nerves. Everyone looked like they were lost in their own secluded world, which gave me more cause for concern. I didn't want my friends to have to carry this burden. Then thankfully, Stride broke the painful silence.

'If there is a way of getting Jimmy into his human state then that would be a great help,' he said.

Draven shook his head from under the blanket. 'That wouldn't make much difference; he will still be an immortal.'

'Yeah, but he'd be easier to handle,' Blaze said still concentrating on the road.

'So, April, you know what to recite?' Stride asked 'I mean, you can read Egyptian right?'

'Of course I can. I'm not studying for a doctorate on Egyptian history and Archaeology for nothing am I? So what exactly is going to happen to you Jyrki? Will you become human?'

'Yes, jeez I haven't really had time to think about this properly. A human?'

'Is it what you really want lad?' Stride asked.

'What I really want? Of course,' I said half-heartedly.

'You don't sound too sure?'

'I do, it's just a lot to take in right now, besides we don't even know if I'm going to win this fight.'

'You've got to; we can't have the human race walking around like zombies for fuck sake,' Stride said.

'Where are we going?' Draven asked

'Stride needs to go back to his place,' Blaze said.

'What's up Stride?' I asked

'I thought I'd do my bit and get some rifles to shoot the bastards.'

'Well, we've only got so much time. They know we have to be there, it's our only chance. If not, those people out there on their way to celebrate Halloween right now, are not gonna know what's hit them,' Blaze said.

'C'mon you lot,' Stride ordered. 'Make sure Draven is covered, we don't want him toasted.'

'Now look, this is probably the only chance we're going get, so let's work out what we're going do later.'

'Do you know what part of Central Park they'll be at?' April said

'Yes by the monument,' Draven said

'What about Ryder? Whose side is he on tonight?'

'I don't really know. I think he feels obligated to Jimmy. I just hope he has some of my Father's wisdom in him though. I see he has your determination Jyrki.'

'If he has your strength and he's on our side then that would be even better, but he's a half breed, so why can't he walk in daylight either?' I said.

'The curse is passed from parent to child, no matter if he's a half breed or not, he still has it in him.'

'Look, I need to know, when do I have to recite this from the book?' April asked.

'Once I've killed Jimmy, I believe. The prophecy will end then, hopefully the Ankh should go back to Mardok and never see the light of day again, pardon the pun.'

144

'I wonder if these wolves can be killed by bullets,' Stride asked, wielding a gun in the air.

'I don't think it's going to be as simple as that somehow,' Blaze said

'Nor me.' I said, pouring a drink.

'The only way to kill them is with the sword, that's the way for all immortal beings,' Draven said.

'Then how did Ryder kill the clan?' April asked

'Yeah that's a good question, how did he? It never really occurred to me until now. That's probably why the prophet couldn't foresee any of this sooner,' I said.

'I think I know how.' Draven said 'I gave his mother a piece of the broken blade. She didn't question my motives, which didn't really surprise me if I'm honest. I said to her if ever I looked any different to her, she was to use it. I'm so sorry Jyrki.'

'It was one thing to leave the compound but to get involve with a human and give her something as precious as that, oh… I just can't fucking believe you,' I said.

'Well in some way it's a good bloody job the mother didn't use it, or we'd be in bigger shite right now.' Stride said.

'Did she know you were a vampire Draven?' April asked

'I think she did, in her own way. Her family was from a long line of Gypsies.'

'Now then, we've only got about 6 hours. What are we gonna do?'

'Oh hell, the band is probably getting ready at the venue, what am I gonna tell them?' Blaze said

'Just tell them an emergency has cropped up, but we will be there,' I said.

Blaze went outside to phone the band.

'Jyrki, can I talk with you a moment, in private?' April said, taking me by surprise.

'Yeah, is there anything wrong?'

'No, come here,' she said

We walked outside and I could sense she was very nervous.

'Jyrki, I know we've only known each other a while, and I know you are a vampire, not that it really matters to me, um,' she looked embarrassed and turned away.' Just incase anything should happen to you tonight, I wanted you to know that I love you. I really do.'

She loves me, this freak of nature. I took her hand and pulled in her close to me. It wasn't that I couldn't say those words back, I wanted to. A part of me was scared to do so.

I caressed her warm, red stained cheek and smiled. She knew I loved her too. I held her in an embrace for few minutes, until Blaze came around the corner.

'Er is everything ok?' he said with a snide grin.

'Um,' I looked at April.

'It's okay man I'm not gonna be mad, in fact I saw this coming. I couldn't be happier for you both.'

'Really?' April said 'You are happy about this? You didn't take to my last boyfriend and he was a lawyer, but it's okay for me to date a vampire?'

'Of course sis, whatever makes you happy.'

He walked back into the warehouse and April rested her head against my chest.

'Why is he so protective, I mean it's not so hard to see why?'

'Because our mother walked out on us when he was fifteen, I was 12.' Her voice began to tremble and she started to cry. 'Our father was away working most of the time and we were left to fend for ourselves. I think Blaze took it upon himself to be the man of the house.'

CHAPTER THIRTY-TWO

Her love for me was more than I could've hoped for, or more than I felt
I deserved. It was going to be a great comfort to me when the time
came to face the wolves of the Apocalypse. At least if anything
happened to me I knew I was worthy of being loved despite my vicious
past. A satisfied smile etched across my face as I watched her walk
back into the warehouse. Whatever evil bound these hounds to the
lowest pits of hell was surely going to feel my wrath.

'Draven!' I yelled.

The sun was drifting quickly behind the horizon. I turned around to
watch it set to the west of the Manhattan skyline, which might well be
for the last time with my own eyes. A deep sadness came over me when
I remembered what the gypsy woman had told me in Helsinki. I so
hoped I wouldn't have sacrifice anything or anyone for my only chance
at being human.

'Brother, what's weighing on your mind?' Draven asked.

I was hesitant to say anything. I looked out onto the water that was now
rapidly changing from a warm orange to a darker blue. I shook my head
in despair. 'It's just something I was told a long time ago. I don't really
want to bother you with it.'

'Just talk to me, let me help.'

'Tonight, there will be a sacrifice for my freedom. I have no idea
what. I was told this by the old gypsy woman back home in Helsinki.'

'That's what's bothering you? Jyrki, you can't let the ramblings of an
old fortune teller overshadow the importance of what tonight means,
and not just for us, but for every being on this earth.'

'But I can trust the ramblings of an ancient prophet?'

'That has more credential and you know it.'

The sun was now completely gone from view and the city lights
flickered on in succession. 'You're right, I know, I guess I needed some
reassurance. So, er, are we both going to tackle this beast then? In full
vampire? It'll be just like the old days.'

'You don't think I'm going to let my little brother save the world all on
his own do you? And take all the credit,' he laughed. 'Of course I'm
going to help. So er, what's the deal with you and April?'

I beamed a toothy smile at Draven. 'She is everything to me. The reason why I want a shot at being human, so then I can love her how she deserves to be loved. I've spent so long on my own and when I finally find someone that loves me for me, no matter what, it all could be just washed away just as quickly as it came.'

'Don't think like that. We will defeat him no matter what it takes. If Father heard you speak like that now, you'd know what he'd say?'

'I think you meant to say, what he'd do.'

Draven laughed. 'Most definitely. The amount of times he has picked me up and slung me half way across the forest for being disobedient.'

'Yes, I remember those days like they were yesterday. Do you ever wonder where he is now?'

'Oh yeah.' he sighed, 'but these days I do not care to ponder on life's little mysteries. It's the now Jyrki, that's all you should be focused on. Maybe the answers are staring us in the face, maybe he is a touch of sunlight that trickles along the water, or maybe he is up there, a flickering of starlight. If things don't go as planned, I just want you to know, it was great to find you again after all this time. Come here,' he said, holding me in an embrace. 'Are you okay? Now, come on let's get this bloody show on the road. I feel like tearing some limbs off tonight,' he said.

'You haven't changed at all bro.'

'Huh, are you sure about that?' he said, looking at his clothes. 'I've spent most my time down the filthy sewers.'

'Blaze, how did it go with the band? Are they alright?'

'Yeah man, we're on around ten, that's if we make it.'

'I'm sure we will, have a little faith in me.'

'It's time.'

'Randulphr? What are you doing here?'

'I thought it would be best to come here for a talk.'

'A talk? About what? I'm about to face a bunch of hounds from hell, and you want to talk, oh look I'm sorry, I'm under a lot of pressure right now.'

'That's quite alright. Mardok sent me.'

'Mardok?' April said. 'Isn't he the prophet?'

'Yes, my dear lady.'

'Well, why can't he tell us what's going to happen?'

'It is not wise to speak of the future before it has happened, despite what others think.'

'So why was the prophecy written?'

'The prophecy is what it is, mere insights into the future, regard them as warnings to steer you on another path, but sometimes one's path is carved out long before they were ever born. Like Jyrki here. Tonight is the night where thousands of years of ancient secrets are about to be exposed that if, you don't stop them first.'

'Which will be the best way to attack them?' Blaze asked

'Hm, well the throat is a good choice. If you can put the blade through his neck and severe his head you might just stand a chance. It also goes for vampires. But, what I'm really here to discuss is Ryder. We have some concern over whether or not he will take their side. Mardok cannot foresee anything, so Jyrki I'm sorry but more than likely you will have to fight him.'

'And the Ankh cannot protect me?'

'No Jyrki, some things just cannot be overwritten. It has done its job this far.'

'And what if Jyrki can't defeat him?' Stride asked, ever the pessimist.

'Then the thin veil that shields this reality from the darkness will be broken. The humans will become hosts for the demons and life here on earth will never be the same again.'

'What sick bastards!' Stride yelled

'Yeah, so come on then. I think we'd better show up before they start attacking people!' Blaze said.

'Slow down boy,' Stride said

'Do you have the book?' Randulphr asked.

'Yes, we do.'

'Then keep it safe, and under no circumstances are you to let it out of your sight. At midnight tonight, it will all be over with so make sure that spell is recited at the first cut with the blade.'

'Why, what will happen?' I asked

'Because Jyrki, they are immortal and this spell is one of the only things which can send them back to where they came from. There is another way though, and that is with the sword. Their blood is precious, like yours. I will tell you something although I'm not really supposed to, but in order for you to understand, I feel it is now necessary. At the very beginning of time, demons roamed the earth. They were its inhabitants for such a long time and it was only when humans began to evolve the war between hell and earth emerged. A battle for possession of earth evolved and is continuing to this day. The ancients as we call them forged a sword, which happens to be the predecessor of the one you hold. It is a very mysterious and sacred sword. Did you also know, the ancient God's your ancestors worshipped once walked the earth, but now reside on an ethereal plane, just like the place you visited in Egypt? Now, Jafar have opened the gates to hell once again and its battle continues, but tonight is the night when it must come to an end one way or the other, as Halloween night is when the veil weakens between their world and this one. You are truly a human Jyrki, but it took an extremely powerful person to bring about the curse which we have protected for millions of years.'

Everyone stood silently outside the warehouse. Even I found it so difficult to take in.

'So, if I don't kill them tonight, it will be like before?'

'Yes, humans will become hosts for these dark spirits. This is also the reason why you had to stay hidden to protect the secrets, until the time came for you to do what you were born to do.'

'Shit, that was heavy. Let us all have a scotch for good luck then,' Stride said. 'Come on, gather around.'

'Now, listen. Raise your glasses in a toast. To friends. Whatever tonight brings, I will still be proud to say that I am glad my father saw what he did that day, because I've never would have met the best bunch of people, and err...vampires,' he laughed 'and I consider every one of you as family. Let's kick these bastards' butts tonight and hope the Gods are smiling down on the human race.'

'Hear hear.'

'Er, I'd like to say something,' Blaze said. 'If I knew what I was talking to that night, I'd never would've invited you back to the party...er, no I'm kidding. Jyrki, you're my best mate and I have every faith in you tonight, best of luck buddy.'

'Thanks. Y'know, back home in Finland, I never thought it was possible I could have friends, let alone live the way I have for the past month. It's been an unforgettable experience. I will do my damnedest tonight for you all.'

'With my help bro.'
'And mine,' April said
I held her hand and smiled.
'So, are we ready?' Randulphr asked
'Hell yeah!'

CHAPTER THIRTY-THREE

'Central Park, here we fucking come!' Draven yelled as we walked back into the warehouse.

'Are you two going out in your vampire costume? It is Halloween,' Stride sniggered. I could see he was half cut on the Scotch again, but tonight of all nights I didn't blame him.

'Of course, but the question is, are you ready to watch a horror show?' I stopped what I was saying; realising April was sitting on the couch. Shit, why did mouth have a tendency to run away with me. 'Um, I didn't mean...'

'It's fine; Don't forget I've seen the real you before haven't I?'

'I know, it's just...well, you know, we've murdered people before and...'

'None of that matters anymore. You are about to repay your debts tonight by facing these things, so that the world will wake up tomorrow and carry on as normal. I believe in you alright, we all do.'

She got up from her seat and walked over towards me. She wrapped her arms around my waist and rested her head onto my chest. I looked over to where Blaze was standing by the cabinet, pouring himself a drink. He raised his glass to me and smiled. I didn't want this moment to end, but I could see Draven was getting impatient.

'Hey Draven, did you fetch the sword from Blaze's place?'

'Yes, it's here,' he said. He pulled open his long brown coat and tapped the handle of the sword attached to his belt. 'It's safe, don't worry.'

'Out of interest, why did you give me the sword? Did you know about any of this?'

'Not really. Father asked me to give it to you for safe keeping the day he came back from the woods with you. He probably knew more than he ever let on to us.'

'Yeah, why doesn't that surprise me?'

'Er, guys I hate to break up the party but um...' Stride said, as he checked his watch. 'It's almost nine. Are you ready?'

'We have no choice to be,' I replied.

'We'll take the van so far, alright? Just across the Brooklyn Bridge to

Time Square,' Blaze said.

'That'll be fine.'

'We should get going,' April said. Looking little anxious. 'I want to get this over with, I can't stand the worrying. What if they have entered our world already?'

'Not possible, it is stated quite clearly in the prophecy. I know of no reason why that should change, so leave the worrying to us, alright?' Draven assured her.

'Ok, I'll just get the book.'

'Let's just get in the van then,' Stride said, as he grabbed his rifle that was hanging on the wall. It wasn't going to be much use, but I didn't want to dash his hopes right now.

I stood by the doorway, watching all my friends scramble about around me. The burden was now almost too much. I flicked off the light switch and closed the door behind me.

We must've been going at least eighty miles an hour across the bridge. I sat back against the van with a mixture of dark thoughts and feelings that I tried to suppress. It was too difficult to speak and so for the journey I chose to remain quiet and calm. I knew when I'd get there I would be on top form. It was the waiting around I couldn't deal with. I was glad the guys respected that.

The van began to slow down. Blaze pulled on the brake and turned the ignition off. Nobody said anything for a minute or two.

'It's not far to walk to the park from here, It'll give us some time to take a breather,' Blaze said.

'Where are we meant to go in the park anyway? I can't remember being told.'

'Bethesda Terrace,' Stride said as he checked the rifle for bullets.

'Why there?'

'It's serving as a portal tonight for the undead and all the evil,' he said. 'I asked that bloody wolf since nobody else did.'

'C'mon then, let's get moving,' Draven tutted. His patience was wearing thin again, as it always did when he was about to face a fight. He pulled open the side door of the van and jumped out.

We walked silently along the sidewalk past all the Halloween celebrations taking place outside the bars and clubs. The sound of laughter and enjoyment was such juxtaposition against what we knew.

If only they knew what was going on a few yards away I wondered.

'Jyrki, are you hungry?' Draven asked with a wicked grin.

'Of course I am,' I smirked. This was just like the old days.

As we stood outside the entrance gate to the park, I watched Draven as he shifted in amongst the shadow of the bushes. He always made it look so damn easy.

'Jyrki! Good luck to ya.'

Stride handed me his pocket- knife and backed away. The vampire I could handle. I just couldn't deal with the shifting part.

'Just do it,' Draven whispered.

I turned sideways to look at April with my own eyes once more and then without thinking too much about it I held the tip of the blade firmly on my right palm and ripped it into the flesh. I snatched a quick glimpse of April standing next to Blaze. She looked frightened despite her heroic speech earlier. Of course, I didn't blame her. The transformation was quick and effortless. Strange how easy it was when you didn't fight against it. Now, I was no longer myself and this had been the worst shifting that has ever happened to me. Draven picked me up off the floor, not that I could remember how I ended up there. His strength was always as powerful as mine was which made me wonder why father had wanted me to keep the Ankh safe.

'You never did take to the shifting did you?' he smiled, flashing his long ivory fangs at me.

'Not as well as some,' I inhaled. 'Human blood?'

Draven gripped me around my arm and looked at me with his fierce looking eyes.

'Don't, you know you can do this. Let's just take a second okay. Think about the real reason why we are here.'

I nodded.

'You're right, in another hour or so we mightn't have to deal with this again.'

'That's the spirit. No more blood cravings; I wonder what that feels like huh?'

I wanted to look at April, but I didn't have the courage. I was so ashamed of my face to do so.

'Jyrki, good luck man,' Blaze said, patting me on the back.

I kept my face turned away from them, even though I desperately wanted to look at April one last time. I flinched as I breathed in the sweet smell of April's perfume as it lingered around me. I felt a slight shiver throughout my body as April's cool hand gently caressed my cheek. She gently edged my face towards her and placed a kiss on my lips. 'Don't forget, whatever happens tonight, I love you,' she said looking up at me.

'I love you too, but nothing is going to change alright. I'll make damn sure it won't,' I said as I backed away from her. I couldn't risk getting too near.

'It's time to go Jyrki. I can sense them.'

'Good luck lads, I'll be firing at the fucking mutts, don't you worry.' Draven stood next to me. Blaze and April were to the far right of the bridge. I glanced down and saw the wolves' shadows slowly elongating out from the arches.

'They're here, just on time.'

I could hear a low snarl and the heaviness of their breath as they paced about below. Another grey wolf walked out and turned around towards us. There were now five of them waiting and I was the only one standing in their way of causing hell on earth.

I flashed a toothy smile towards April, hoping this wouldn't be the last I'd see of her. She raised her hand gently as if it was a goodbye and sought comfort against Stride's chest. My nostrils flared as I could now smell the deathly stench of the wolves below. I leaned over the bridge and saw them walking smugly around the monument. Now I was angry and I could sense my demon was as twice as powerful as it ever been. All the self-doubt I had earlier soon diminished.

I was just about to jump but something told me to look behind Blaze and April. It was Randulphr and Father. I wasn't sure if the image was in my mind or real but I felt empowered by the thought that my father was looking on.

'Time to end the prophecy,' I heard. I held the sword tightly and climbed over the railings onto the edge of the bridge. The wolves snarled below and I could almost taste the evil that emanated from them. As I looked around the park there was still no sign of Ryder.

'Draven, where's Ryder?' I whispered.

'No idea, we'll sort him out later, c'mon let's send these back to where they came from.'

'What are you waiting for? Afraid are you?' Jimmy laughed
'It's you who should be afraid.'

I jumped off the bridge and in an instant, I landed upright on my feet inches away from the mouth of the foul smelling breath of Jimmy. I backed away, still keeping a firm eye on them for any sudden movement.

Two of the wolves began walking around Draven. I reached for the sword from my side and wielded it in the air. The wolf stopped and I saw the fear magnify in its eyes. But it didn't stop him. He ran towards me as I gave a forceful swing of the blade.

'Every last one,' I heard in my head.

The blade just gashed his leg as he stumbled and fell beside me. I snatched a quick look at Draven, he was tackling the wolf with his bare hands. Our speed might be our saving grace.

'Jyrki look out,' April yelled from the bridge.

The smallest wolf of the pack came charging up; I ran straight towards it and punctured him through the gut. It was almost too easy. One down. Jimmy still wasn't letting up; I wanted to help Draven who at this point was taking a beating. If they gashed his neck I thought, he'd be gone.

'Leave him,' I screamed. I must've diverted the wolf's attention, giving Draven a chance. He gripped the wolf around his neck and threw him against the Angel statue.

'Arghh!' Jimmy had pounced on my back. I fell forwards on all fours, gripping my fingernails into the concrete floor as I felt the flesh on my back being torn apart by Jimmy's claws. 'I'm trapped, It's all over,' I whimpered.

'Get up,' Randulphr spoke.

I felt a release of the weight on my back and the coldness of the concrete beneath me.

'That's another one gone back to hell. Come on, get up!' Draven shouted.

I could now feel the trickling of the blood running down my back. I must carry on, I thought.

'You ok bro? Go after Jimmy. I'll keep this other one away ok.'
I looked up and nodded.

'Two down, two to go,' Draven hollered.

156

'Send him to me once I'm done with him alright?'

The two wolves paced about, biding their time, watching us carefully with their intense glare.

I can do this. I ran towards them, hoping to take them unawares. The other wolf went straight for Draven. I held Jimmy by the throat and slammed him down onto the floor.

'It's time to say goodnight.'

'You think so, do you? This isn't the last of it, there's worse to come,' he grinned.

I took one look at him and pushed the sword into his stomach. I let out a gasp and wiped my brow. Unnervingly his words were still lingering in my mind

'Jyrki!'

I snapped out of my thoughts and turned to face Draven. The wolf was now on top of him watching every move I took. It was almost as if everything around me had drowned itself out. I was in a moment that I had always feared. It took my mind back to Finland when I saw their ashes blow away in the snowdrift. What was I to do? I clenched the sword tightly and thought of taking it by surprise. Would I get there in time? It was less than 5 yards away.

Draven tilted his head towards me as the moonlight highlighted his blue eyes. He laid there, quite still, looking at me as if it was a goodbye, but I was not ready to say goodbye to him again. All that kept going through my head was that I must try to get us both out of this mess alive. But how? I couldn't focus on anything. The wolf was now standing on top of him and I was certain he smirked at me as he lowered his head towards Draven's neck. I knew he was enticing me to make a quick move, but I am far too smart to fall for his tricks, besides, my body was in some kind of shock and I could not shift out of the uncomfortable position I was in on the floor. As I shifted my gaze from Draven towards the trees, I could see something heading towards me in mid-air. The next thing I knew the wolf was lying down on the floor, dead.

They were all gone. Just like that.

The prophecy was now surely broken. I felt my chest and looked down where the Ankh should've been resting. A twinge of sadness swept over me as I realised this was the start of a new beginning as a mortal. I turned around and raised my eyes up towards the bridge and there stood April reciting an Ancient Egyptian text.

I lowered my head to my knees, allowing the old language to envelope me, as if it were washing away my sins. I bent over slightly, arching my back that was still stinging from my wounds. I let out a sigh with relief that it was all over, but somehow I didn't feel any different. Not yet.

I could hear Stride hollering something at me as he came running down the steps towards me, but with all that was going through my head I could not quite make out what he was saying. Everything that had happened tonight somehow felt like a dream. I was weak, exhausted and in a lot of pain, but at least Draven was still there. I got to my feet and walked over to him. Something didn't seem right. I knelt down beside him when my hands began to shake. He was still looking at me, but there was no life in his eyes.

'Oh no, Draven don't you dare die on me…'

I turned him over onto his side and saw the wolf had taken a bite out of his neck, draining him of his blood. I should've known what they were capable of. 'This cannot be happening to me again,' I wept. I could hear the faint tapping of the rain as it converged with the water in the fountain next to me. I placed Draven back on to the ground and walked towards the statue. The rain belted down hard and the Angel looked as if she was crying, sharing my pain.

Stride rested a hand on my shoulder, which prompted me glance up over the park. I saw a dark figure approaching me and waited anxiously at who it could be.

'Ryder…' I whispered.

I noticed his eyes widened as he looked in Draven's direction, and as I glanced down again where he was laying, he had gone.

'You threw the sword?' I said

'Yes, he was my father.'

I looked towards Stride, who had a tear in his eye.

'I'm sorry lad, I'm really sorry. I loved him like a son.'

'Jyrki, has it worked? Are you any different yet?' April cried

'I really don't know,' I said, I was in pain and now I had lost my brother for the second time. It was far too much to comprehend.

CHAPTER THIRTY-FOUR

'A sacrifice. Just like she said.'

I dropped the sword on the floor. It fell, clattering as it hit the concrete. I stood amongst the aftermath of a whirlwind of an event that didn't seem quite real to my mind just yet. As I lifted my arm to my face to wipe away my tears, I became alerted to the smell of their blood, which had stained my hands. I pulled it away immediately and looked down. The front of my body was drenched in red. A cold wind had picked up rustling the trees around us, breaking the silence. It was only then I had looked and realised the wolves bodies had disappeared.

'Er, Jyrki? What about him?' Stride pointed to Ryder. 'What shall we do with him? Is he harmless?'

I had completely forgotten about Ryder standing there.

I raised my eyes in his direction. He stood a few yards from the statue staring at me with a fearful look on his face. As if he was expecting me to lash out at him. I eased up my stance a touch and brushed my hair away that had become stuck to my face with the blood. How could I hurt him? He was the image of Draven and if that was not enough, he was the only family I had left. It was then the realisation hit me. I was human.

'The Ankh has gone,' April said.

'Does that mean you're now human?' Blaze asked.

'And him. Is he human now?' Stride asked again with a little anxiousness.

'Ryder, come over here,' I said. 'What about you? Are you any different?'

He walked nervously towards me and nodded.

'So it's been broken? No more vampire?' I exclaimed.

It sounded almost too good to be true. Over a hundred years and with most of that spent on the run, I sunk to the floor in merciful relief, completely content with the fact that the human race were spared from the apocalypse. Although my body was aching with exhaustion, I sat back against the Angel fountain and smiled.

'I guess this means you're my nephew right?'

I looked up towards Ryder standing there. He was very much on edge.

'Yes, but I wouldn't blame you if you didn't want to know me.'

My head wasn't ready to deal with all the details right now. I was well aware he had killed the clan, but what could I possibly do to him. He was family - my only family.

'Then family sticks together. Are you with me?'

'Of course,' he smiled, looking relieved.

'Then I'll introduce you to your new family. Guys, come and meet Ryder.'

'Alright son,' Stride said looking slightly spooked by the likeness.

'This is April, my... girlfriend.'

'We've already met at the hotel,' she said.

'And Blaze. My good friend and fellow band member.'

'Alright mate,' Blaze said.

April knelt down beside me on the floor. I pulled her in close to me and kissed her on the forehead.

'So how does it feel to be human?'

My back was in pain but I managed to force a smile.

'Better with you,' I whispered.

'Here, let me help you up,' Blaze said, 'I'm really sorry about Draven. He was a good guy, for a vampire.'

'Thanks. I suppose I shouldn't be too surprised,' I said, remembering what the gypsy woman had told me.

'I hate to ask at a time like this but are you up to the gig. You know, you really don't have to?'

I was covered in blood and I felt like shit. 'Of course I am. The band means just as much to me y'know. It kept me going.'

'Wow. What a fucking night eh?' Stride huffed as we walked out of Central Park.

'Yep, at least the sun will still shine tomorrow,' I said.

April clenched my hand tightly and rested her head against my arm.

'I'm so glad this is all over. I'm going to cancel the exhibition tomorrow and book a holiday.'

'A holiday would be nice as long as it's not Egypt. So do you have the last piece of the prophecy with you?'

'Yes, it's safe don't worry. Why?'

160

'Because I think I'd like to know what's in it, wouldn't you.'

'Are you sure? I think it's best not to know.'

'Well, after tonight, I think you may be right.'

'So from now on then Halloween has another meaning for us I guess,' Blaze said.

'It certainly has. It shall now be known as the night of the undead. So are we still playing tonight?'

'Yes, in half hour. Once you cleaned yourself up. We're not a black metal band y'know.'

We walked a few blocks down the road to the venue. Izzy was standing outside the back entrance waiting for us.

'Where the fuck have you been?' he said

'Oh just finishing off some business. We're here now anyway, so chill out,' I said pushing the door open.

'You're full of blood? This wasn't part of the act was it?' Izzy said, looking perplexed.

'No,' Blaze said, 'I changed my mind about that on the way here. Oh Jyrki, I left your stuff in here alright,' he said as he opened the door to the changing room. 'I'll be at the bar ok. I could murder some pints now.'

Blaze left the room, closing the door shut behind him. I had only just removed all of my bloody clothing when there was a tap at the door.

'Jyrki, is it okay if I come in?'

'Ryder! Of course you can.'

'Um, I wanted to say thanks for, you know, being alright with everything.'

'That's ok. Do you want talk? I think we have some catching up to do?'

'Yeah, I'd like that.'

I could see there was more worrying him. The way he stood nervously with his hands in his pockets, and how he glanced around the room; unable to look at me for all the guilt he kept inside for all these years. Part of me was feeling very sorry for him.

'What's wrong? You know you can talk to me don't you?'

'I...I just feel guilty, about you know...'

'That you killed the clan? Oh sorry, I didn't mean for it come out like that.'

'No, you're right and you have every reason to be angry with me. I did kill the clan, but I was made to do it. It wasn't because I wanted to kill them as I knew they were different, just like me. Jimmy found me when I was five years old wandering in the woods. I was his connection to the Ankh he kept telling me. I didn't know what he meant by this but one day I started asking questions about who my father was. Stupidly he told me everything, even what he was planning on doing. So, that day at the compound, I overheard someone call Draven. He was standing just feet away from me. Immediately I knew he was my father. Well, what could I do, I had to save his life. So without Jafar seeing anything I picked up the nearest thing I could see and knocked him unconscious. I then hid him under a mound until I could go back for him later. My loyalties may have looked like they were with Jimmy, but they weren't.'

'Okay, I suppose it couldn't had been easy for you either, so let the past be alright. There's nothing we can do about it now.'

I returned to the sink to continue trying to scrub all the blood from my hands when I felt a nudge on my arm. I looked down and Ryder was holding out his palm.

'I still have this.'

I looked at him, and then down towards his hand again, he was holding out a piece of a blade.

'The sword?'

'Yes, I thought you may want it.'

I took it out of his palm and wrapped it in my blood-stained shirt. It was after all Draven's favourite thing he possessed.

'I'm sorry you didn't get a chance to know Draven…he was a very special person that deserved more than the life he led offered him.'

'I'm thankful I managed to save his life that day, it was the least I could do. I'm just sorry I couldn't save your dad.'

'Yeah, well I still don't know what happened to him. He wasn't there at the compound when I saw them all turn to dust. Anyway, enough of that talk for now. Would you pass me my jacket?' I asked.

'Ready?' Blaze shouted from the doorway.

'Always.'

'Oh hey,' he said opening the door again, 'you'll never guess who's here? Jules. I called her a few nights ago. Which was a mad thing to do when we didn't even know if things were gonna turn out okay. Well, see you out by the bar, there's a Guinness waiting for ya,' he said quite happily.

'Nice one, I'll be out in a second, ok.'

'C'mon you, I guess you can keep the girls away from the stage, make yourself useful.' I sniggered.

'Sure uncle. I can call you that right?'

'Jyrki is better. I reckon uncle makes me sound old.'

The bar was full tonight, which wasn't much of a surprise as we had gained quite a following in the city. I looked out over the sea of heads to find April and Stride talking by the bar. I walked up behind April and put my arm around her.

'Ah here he is, our new human friend.'

'Stride, I just want to thank you for everything...'

'Now, now lad, I'm just glad to help, but I will be sorry to say goodbye.'

'Goodbye? Why?' I said feeling quite stunned.

'Well, you see, I still have some business I've got to sort out so I was thinking of going travelling for a bit on the old girl...'

'What's the old girl?' April laughed.

'It's my motorcycle love, what did you think I meant?'

'Just remember, you'll always be welcome here.' I said

'So you're staying in New York then?'

I looked at April.

'Well, for now at least.'

'It's good to see you happy, and you have a bit more colour in them cheeks. You look after him love, he's something special.'

'I will do, you can count on that,' April said.

CHAPTER THIRTY-FIVE

There was one thing I had not quite thought about since becoming human and that was I was no longer an immortal. Here I was, sitting in a room full of people knowing that anyone at any time could cause me harm. Not that I thought they would want to, but I was feeling quite vulnerable with all these new emotions that were attacking my mind. I certainly didn't feel like the human I was when I went back to Egypt. This was different.

'Oh you'll soon get use to this,' Stride said.
I watched him stump out his fourth cigarette in the half hour we sat here. I never really thought to ask what the point in it was.

'What exactly am I going to get use to?'

'Being a human of course. You don't have to pretend with me, I can see you're looking a little startled by it all.

'Yeah, it is kind of overwhelming. I only wish Draven could've been here too.'

'I can imagine so. Just remember there isn't one person in this room who isn't fucked up in some way or another. Nobody's perfect lad just be yourself and you'll be fine.'

'It's...oh doesn't matter,' I shook my head wishing I hadn't said anything. The subject matter was something I've always tried to avoid discussing, but now it was inevitable.

'No, no, we're not letting this go. What's bothering you? Spill it. Tell your uncle Stride.'
I sighed and put my drink down. This certainly wasn't an easy topic to discuss.

'Mortality,' I said looking down at my half-drunken glass. 'The fear of being hurt or worse. I guess I haven't had time to give it much thought until now.'

'Don't go worrying over things which may or may never happen. You have been given a second chance, Jyrki. Embrace it. Now the curse has gone and the wolves have fucked off back to hell or whatever they came from, you start living, if anyone deserves it, you do,' he said pointing at me.

'Thanks Stride. You know from the moment I first met you I always thought you were a crazy fucker, but you've come to be a father figure to me. I don't know what I would've done without your help.'

'Now that's where you've gone wrong already. Never suck up to anyone!' he laughed. 'That's rule number one my friend.'

'Unless they were paying you!' Blaze said. 'You'll never guess what? We've been offered a support slot with a well-known Glam band in Europe,' he said leaning over the table. See that guy over there?' he pointed across the room towards a guy with long blonde hair and eyeliner, 'he's offering us a couple of months' worth of gigs, how about it?'

'In Europe?' My jaw dropped and I looked towards Stride.

'Yeah, Just a thought, do you even have a passport?' Blaze said. Stride slammed down his drink on the table and laughed hysterically. I looked at Blaze with a wide grin across my face.

'Um, nope,' I couldn't help but laugh either.

'You mean to say you don't have one at all. How did you get to New York then?'

'How do you think? By cargo ship of course.'

He shook his head at me disgustingly and walked over to the bar.

The Halloween theme was quite apt for tonight. I chuckled to myself at the blatant display of fetish bunny girls and vamped up Goths, making me feel slightly out of place since the curse had gone, but it was all pleasing to the eye nonetheless.

April leaned in next to me and whispered in my ear. 'Ryder is staying with Blaze tonight, so you can come back to mine...if you want this is?'

'Absolutely,' I said, cupping her head in my hands, 'but you know my back is in bits don't you?'

'I'm sure I can sort it out for you.'

'Hey, hey come on break it up you two; let's get on that fucking stage. Oh and having Ryder around is going to be handy with all this shifting of gear. I might give him a job,' Blaze said as he walked past the table with Jules.

'Oh hey Jyrki, it's nice to see you again,' she said.

I raised my hand and nodded at her.

'Looks like things are working out just fine,' Stride said, lighting another cigarette.

'Yeah, I hope they stay that way too.'

The show ended to a rapturous applause. As I was now in a human state I began to feel the strain a touch more, or so I thought until I saw Ryder helping Blaze with the equipment. I looked inquisitively at him. He showed tremendous strength still. I shrugged and put the thought to the back of mind. The majority of the audience had gone home and the bartender was busily wiping down the glasses behind the bar. Just as I was about to bend down to pick up Blaze's amp, I felt a tugging on my arm.

'Hey, any chance of signing this for me?'

'You want an autograph?' I said, looking up at her. She looks good enough to eat. Shit, what in the hell am I thinking.

I removed my sunglasses and put them inside my jacket pocket. The young woman with long blonde hair and dressed in a tight fitting PVC suit handed me a notebook and a pen. I was feeling slightly uncomfortable with her staring at me and flirting so I quickly scribbled my name and handed it back to her.

'Here you go. I'll see you at the next gig right?'

'For sure,' she giggled and walked off.

'Groupies already?' April said

'All part of the job,' I joked 'Come here,' I said pulling her towards me. 'Are ready to go home?'

'I've been waiting to hear that for a long time.'

'Not as long as I have.'

CHAPTER THIRTY-SIX

It had been a long night and I was reeling with a mixture of emotions. Part of me felt unsure of whether the curse had been broken. It all seemed too easy for my liking. I needed to snap out of these negative thoughts. I had lost Draven tonight and for that reason only I ought to be thankful for my life, not wallow in self-pity.

'April. Are you ready?' I called. She was saying goodbye to some friends by the bar. I noticed the blonde male looked over at me peculiarly and whispered something to April. An uneasy feeling came over me. Then I noticed April turned to look at me with a wide smile and whispered something back to the bloke. Pangs of jealousy I guessed. Must have been a new human emotion I was experiencing.

'Hey. Are you coming back to mine then?' She said as she walked over to me standing by the doorway.

'Sure, if that's what you really want?'
I smiled at her as I tilted my head down to her level. She leaned in close and kissed me on the cheek.

'Of course it is.'

'Um, so who is he then?' I nodded to the guy.

'What are you talking about? The blonde guy I was talking too?'

'Yeah, him. He was looking at me rather oddly.'

'Jealous are you?' she laughed. 'For your information that was one of my colleagues, James. He fancied you.'

'What?'

'Don't look so shocked, you're a good looking guy. He's gay by the way, er you do know what that is don't you?' she said, laughing at me.

'Um...'

'Well, anyway don't worry, I put him straight,' she said, laughing even more. She looked at me as if she was expecting me to 'get' the joke. 'Oh come on,' she grabbed my arm, 'let's say goodbye to Stride before he leaves.'
I put my arm around April's shoulder and walked out the door to the sight of Blaze and Stride talking by the van.

'So, er, are you two are off then?' Stride asked.

'Yeah, it's been a long day. So where are you going now?'

'Oh, I'm gonna start packing soon, make my way back to Blighty. I've quite missed my local pub and my wife.'

'You have a wife?' I said surprised.

'Yeah, didn't I ever talk to you about her?'

I flicked a look at Blaze who looked just as surprised as I was.

'No,' I shrugged.

'Noreen her name is, a fine woman. She makes the best haggis in Glasgow. I'll have to introduce you one day.'

'Of course, I look forward to it. You're still full of surprises aren't you?' I joked

'Absolutely, you've got to keep life interesting pal,' he said taking his hand from his jacket pocket. I shook his hand and I was almost sure he had a tear in his eye.

'It's been a helluva ride hasn't it?'

'It has, but I couldn't have done it without you.'

'You'll keep in touch yeah?'

'Of course, we'll have a reunion every Halloween. Uh, Blaze…we're leaving now ok?'

'Yeah sure, I'll call around tomorrow to pick you up.'

'Ryder?'

'Yeah?'

'I'll call you tomorrow?' I shouted, but he seemed more preoccupied with the women that had gathered around him. I decided to leave him to it.

For once, the rain had stopped as we walked back to April's place a few blocks away. I held her hand as we walked silently through the crowds gathered outside a theatre holding a masquerade ball. I brushed past vampires and devils thinking this could've been the norm right now. I shuddered at the thought. After the night we had neither of us felt like talking much, and I was happy with that, it was just so good to be in April's company for a change.

April let go of my hand and stopped outside a townhouse.

'This is home, well, part of it. I live on the third floor,' she said, gesturing towards the house.

I watched her walk up the steps towards the red door when I thought I had heard something whispering to me. The tree behind me on the sidewalk rustled in a sudden gust of wind that had come from nowhere,

which propelled me to glance around the quiet street. I had no idea
what I was hoping to uncover or any idea as to why I should've been
bothered. The curse had been lifted.

'Are you ok?' she called.

'Yeah. I think so.'

I could tell she was nervous by the way her hand shook as she opened
the lock.

We both knew what would happen tonight, it was inevitable. The
attraction between us was instant from the moment we first met. It was
a wonder how it had taken us this long to arrive at this point.

'Are you coming in? It's not like I have to invite you in now, since
you're not a vampire anymore,' she smiled.

'Very funny, you shouldn't watch those vampire movies you know,
they got us all wrong.'

'Ah, I take it you've been watching Blaze's DVD collection. So
what's your favourite?'

I rested my arm on the metal handrail and thought about the question
for a few seconds. 'That would have to be Scars of Dracula, with
Christopher Lee. He portrays the character in a very cool and suave
way, but it's also fascinating how he converses with people--'

'Woah, slow down,' she laughed, 'sounds like you've taken a degree
on the subject. Which sounds like a good idea though, I mean, have you
decided what you're going to do incase the band don't work out?'

'It sounds like you don't have a lot of faith in your brother?'

'Oh you know what I mean. It's always a good idea to have something
to fall back on that's all.'

'Of course, but... I need to live for a while, you do understand that
don't you?'

Under the security light that flickered on, I noticed her cheeks flushed a
hint of pink and saw the warmth in her eyes as she gazed down at me.

'Yeah, I do understand, I'm sorry. I'm getting ahead of myself.'

'You need to live a little too from what I have seen.'

Feeling quite nervous, I walked up the steps to the front door. She
placed her hand in mine and led me through the hallway. I drew a sharp
breath in excitement as she slipped her hands under my shirt and pulled
me against her body. I eased her gently against the wall before stooping
down to kiss her. I clasped her face in my hands. 'I love you,' I

whispered before slowly moving my hands down her curves.

'Love you too,' she smiled, as she nodded towards the stairs.

I found it impossible to keep my hands off her as we walked up the steep staircase to her apartment. The hall was dark and April fumbled around for the light switch. 'Must be nerves,' she said 'I don't usually forget things so easily.'

'Am I that much of a distraction?' I laughed.

'You have no idea, seriously.'

Whether it was the excitement of the evening or not I don't know, but I could feel my throat burning. Like when I use to crave blood. I smiled at her and leaned against the doorframe, watching her as she looked for the keys in her handbag; when I realised I was no longer looking at her as myself but as the thing I used to be.

It must be my mind playing tricks. The curse was broken; I was not a vampire anymore. I snapped out of my dark thoughts thinking it was probably some sort of after effect of the curse, but was it. My heart beated but did it beat new blood?

'Hey Jyrki, I'm not going to charge you an entry fee y'know.'

'Oh sorry, I was...'

'That's alright, I know it's been a tough night...oh Merlin, there you are!'

She looked over towards the sofa and I wondered whom she was talking too.

'Merlin?'

'It's my cat,' she said

I saw a black head and two green eyes peeping at me from behind the black leather sofa. I knelt down to call the cat over but he just looked at me and hissed.

'Hm, he doesn't like me?' I joked.

'Eat him,' I heard a whisper.

'Um...did you hear that?' I said, as I shot up from the floor.

'Hear what?'

'Oh it doesn't matter,' I said, feeling like an idiot. Although I was certain I heard something.

'He's quite nervous with new people,' she said as she picked the cat up. 'I'll just give him some food, make yourself comfortable.'

'It's a nice place,' I said as I removed my jacket and walked over to the book cabinet. The shelf covered almost the whole wall. I ran my fingers across the leather binds fascinated by the titles she had on there.

'I take it you like reading then?'

'Absolutely. I did a lot in Finland, so I knew--'

'Shhh.'

She came over and wrapped her arms around me.

'So where were we?' she whispered seductively in my ear.

'Hm, I think I was about here,' I said, as I bent down to kiss her.

'Do you want to go into the bedroom?'

She led me into her room and placed the small bedside lamp on.

'I won't be a moment. I want this to be just right...'

I watched her as she walked over to her ivory vanity table by the window and pulled out four candles from the drawer. Almost instantly, the air in the room filled with the sweet scent of vanilla. I took this moment to sit down on the silky crimson duvet and with jittery hands; removed my shoes. In the background, I heard the faint relaxing sound of Celtic music coming from the speakers. For once, I felt relaxed as I leaned back on the bed, when I could feel two warm hands gently massaging my shoulders. I breathed in deeply and closed my eyes. Slowly she ran her hands down my chest and one by one opened the buttons on my shirt. 'Come here...' I whispered. I held her hand and turned around to face her on the bed. She smiled at me with her red lips as I brushed her dark hair back that fell over her breasts. I had noticed the warmth of the candlelight illuminated a sexy glow to her face just when I felt her hands reach down to my crotch and unzipped the fly on my jeans. I pulled her in close to my flesh and wrapped my legs around her body. She tilted her head to the side inviting me to press a tender kiss on her neck. I wanted her in more ways than she could ever have known. The voice was still quite dominant in my head but I suppressed the urge to taste her the way I wanted to when I saw her that night at the bar. Now our bodies were intertwined she sighed excitedly as I slid my hands down her back and unhooked her red lace bra.

My eyes flickered open to the sound of the morning New York traffic outside. I glanced around the room; I must've slept like a human last night I thought, despite the odd feeling of craving blood. I felt relaxed and content amongst the red silk bed sheets knowing April was by my side. I had just turned over to look at April when a piercing of light that came through the crack in the curtain singed my face.

'What the fuck!' I yelled covering my head with the duvet. 'April, don't open the curtains whatever you do.' I said, almost startling her.

'Why, what's wrong?' she said sounding half asleep.

'I don't know yet, but it can't be good,' I said; feeling spun out.
The phone started ringing, and I flinched. 'Answer it, it may be Blaze,' I said.
April sat upright on the bed and answered the phone.

'Oh Blaze, what's wrong now?' She said as she checked her alarm clock. 'Do you realise it's only 7.45 in the am…on a Sunday?' She sighed. 'Here,' she said, handing me the receiver. 'It's Blaze. My God, I swear you two are like a married couple on times.'

'Something has happened and you're not gonna believe it…' I blurted out.

'Well you're not gonna believe this either, it's Ryder! He's gone.'

'Gone? What do you mean by that?
'No idea, he must've took off before it got light. There is a note addressed to you though.'

'Is there? Well, I have another problem right now. I am not sure if the curse really was broken last night?'

'What are you talking about?'

'Well, how do I put this, oh I know…I was almost turned to fucking dust just now.'

'What the fuck. I'll be over in ten minutes alright. Just don't make a move until I get there.'
Blaze hung up and as I bent over the bed to put the receiver back, I saw something glistening by the lamp.

'Oh shit!' I said, nudging April awake again.

'The Ankh is here.'

3353501R00094

Printed in Great Britain
by Amazon.co.uk, Ltd.,
Marston Gate.